Weaponized Honor: Tactical Love

Marios Ellinas

Son of Thunder Publications

Copyright © Marios Ellinas
& Son of Thunder Publications 2017

Author: Marios Ellinas
www.mariosellinas.com/books

Published by Son of Thunder Publications Ltd 2017
www.sonofthunderpublications.org

Cover concept by Gabrial Heath of Aspect Reference Design.
Cover adaptation by Derina Lucas, www.derinalucasdesigns.com

Page art graphic support by Iain Gutteridge of I.G. Design
www.ig-graphic-design.co.uk

Formatted by Avocet Typeset, Somerton, Somerset TA11 6RT
www.avocet-typeset.com

All rights reserved. This book is protected by the copyright laws of the United States of America and the United Kingdom. This book may not be copied or reprinted for commercial gain or profit. The use of short quotations or occasional page copying for personal or group study is permitted and encouraged. Beyond small sections and single pages, permission to reproduce this material for group study can be requested from either the author or the publisher.

Published in the United Kingdom
for world-wide distribution

ISBN
978-1-911251-21-7 (print)
978-1-911251-22-4 (ebook)

Unless otherwise indicated, all scripture quotations
are taken from the New King James Version®.
Copyright © 1982 by Thomas Nelson. Used by permission.
All rights reserved.

Scripture quotations marked (TLB) are taken from The Living Bible
copyright © 1971. Used by permission of Tyndale House Publishers, Inc.,
Carol Stream, Illinois 60188. All rights reserved.

Scriptures marked VOICE™ are taken from The Voice.
Copyright© 2008 by Ecclesia Bible Society. Used by permission.
All rights reserved.

Scripture marked TPT are taken from The Passion Translation.
Copyright © 2004 by Holman Bible Publishers, Nashville, Tennessee.
All rights reserved.

Author's Note of Thanks

My heartfelt thanks to the Revelation Partners team for editing the manuscript and to Rachel Hall for her professional editing expertise, Gabrial Heath and Derina Lucas for the cover design, Iain Gutteridge for the page art, Paul Medcalf for the formatting, the Son of Thunder Publications team for the transcription of my talks, Heather Rayner for believing in this work and for outstanding communication, Son of Thunder Publications for our collaboration and the many volunteers – can't wait to meet you all! Ian Clayton for being a great friend and mentor. Danielle, Christos, Caleb, and Chloe—the best family I could have hoped for. The leaders and congregation of Valley Shore for their constant support. My parents for their unconditional love and for always having my back.

Marios Ellinas
Connecticut, USA
December 2017

Table of Contents

Introduction	9
Chapter 1 Honor as a Verb	15
Chapter 2 Best Laid Plans	25
Chapter 3 Kingdom of Honor	33
Chapter 4 Woman: God's Secret Weapon	43
Chapter 5 Painting Targets	53
Chapter 6 Redemption Through Honor	61
Chapter 7 The Anatomy of Apology	77
Chapter 8 Dirges for Spear-Throwers	87
Chapter 9 Honor's Rewards	97
Epilogue	109
Author's Bio	111

INTRODUCTION

"For the weapons of our warfare are not carnal but mighty in God for pulling down strongholds" (2 Corinthians 10:4).

Honor is a powerful weapon in our spiritual arsenal—not for destruction, but for redemption.

* * *

Well-chosen language such as 'spiritual warfare' has the ability to make abstract concepts intriguing and easy to understand. Such is the case with the phrase *spiritual warfare:* it communicates the idea that the sons of God on the earth are engaged in a cosmic battle between YHVH's[1] forces and those from the kingdom of darkness. The battle rages in the invisible realm, but military imagery and terminology from the physical realm brings it into focus—armies, strategies, battlefields, weapons, causes, soldiers, generals, and more. Scripture lends much support and confirmation to the notion. Paul said, *"For we do not wrestle against flesh and blood, but against principalities, against powers, against the rulers of the darkness of this age, against spiritual hosts of wickedness in the heavenly places"* (Ephesians. 6:12). For centuries now, followers of Jesus Christ have memorized, quoted, preached, sung, and rallied around such verses and

---

[1] YHVH are the Hebrew letters used in the Bible for the name of God – Yahweh

the idea that we are part of an eternal and victorious army. We have launched church programs, prayer gatherings, conferences, and entire ministries on the assumption that we are God's warriors, battling and prevailing against the enemy.

The concept certainly works for us. With great passion and fervency, we charge ahead. We hold onto the promise of our Christ-wrought ultimate victory, as well as the biblical affirmation that we are overcomers by the blood of the lamb (Revelation 12:11) and "more than conquerors" (Romans 8:37). Through our valiant efforts, many victories have been won and much good is being spread throughout the whole earth. And yet, if we are fully honest, the outcomes of many of our confrontations against enemy forces have not been favorable. The product of our spiritual warring hasn't always matched the assurances of victory made in pre-battle pep talks and bold declarations from pulpits. We can claim to be victorious in as many ways as we can imagine: however, the truth is inescapable—most Christ-followers neither look nor act as winners.

We do not need to go far beyond the Church itself to find proof. More Christian homes than we care to count are riddled with rebellion, division, even divorce. Parents trade family-time and values—even their very souls—for their careers. Hidden lifestyles and erroneous mindsets lurk behind closed doors. Couples pretend to have it all together, while striving to guard dark secrets, such as pornography addictions, substance abuse, and marital infidelity. Local churches and ministries have issues as well. We find leaders driven by the fear of man; belief systems saturated with religiosity; congregations riddled by competitiveness, insecurity, rejection, and striving; entire movements dominated by the multi-faceted fabrications of church politics—what Jesus warned against as *"the leaven of Herod"* (Mark 8:15) Consequently, we face the crisis of masses of believers who are fed up with the Church. The best case

INTRODUCTION

scenario has such individuals and families leaving peacefully and honorably, doing their utmost not to harm the body at large by avoiding head-on collisions with church leaders. The worst cases, however, have people leaving the church bitter and disillusioned, then wandering from one spiritual desert to the next, hoping that the church oasis up ahead will be better than the place they left.

What happened to our victory? Why such heavy losses inflicted on so many different fronts? We haven't been wrong in recognizing we are fighting spiritual battles, and we are not lacking for loyalty or commitment to our cause. I believe the problem has to do with the weapons we have been using and the battlefields on which we have been choosing to fight. Though we have over-quoted the verses pertaining to us not wrestling with flesh and blood, we have been engaging the forces of the enemy with physical means, not spiritual: we have been engaging the forces on earth, not in Heaven.

Yet for the battle to be won, it must be fought on God's battlefield—in celestial realms, not terrestrial. And the weapons of our warfare must not be carnal, but *"mighty in God for pulling down strongholds" (*2 Corinthians 10:4).

We have been taught that David ran towards Goliath armed only with a slingshot and five smooth stones: true, but not the whole truth. When the giant saw David charging forth, he asked, "Am I a dog that you come at me with sticks?" What sticks did Goliath see, and where did they come from? Psalm 23:4 may provide the answer. Here we find David declaring that God's "rod and staff" comfort him, that YHVH prepares a table in the presence of his enemies. Perhaps the sticks Goliath perceived were really the rod and staff of God protecting David.

David was not fighting Goliath, or any battle for that matter with carnal means. His weapons came from the heavenly realm he had learned to navigate through his intimate relationship with YHVH. Could it be that in confronting Goliath, David was wielding the rod of Aaron and the staff of Moses—objects made from wood, but infused with supernatural authority and power? And that he was contending not from a place of striving but from a seat of rest, with absolute trust in the power of God working in him? We have yet more evidence from the Psalms, where David writes: "He prepares a table before me in the presence of my enemies" (Psalm 23:5).

Our strongest arsenal in spiritual warfare is love and honor is the most significant weapon in that arsenal. As a weapon, honor is both offensive and defensive in nature. When it is wielded with a heart fully committed to God and to His ways, honor unleashes heavenly intervention in our earthly encounters. And, it secures comprehensive and lasting victory.

Weaponized Honor presents the strategic value of honor, the way by which Heaven co-labors with humanity to leverage love in a tactical manner for spiritual warfare. We will examine portions of the lives of David, Daniel, Esther and others to demonstrate through scriptural examples a particular pattern, that of God's Sons (men and women alike) releasing love and YHVH unleashing Heaven into circumstances wherein His children and purposes are challenged. When we engage our enemies with honor, we activate Heaven on our behalf. We do our part from a seat of rest and God's angels are sent to settle the score. Thus, our loving stance through honor is leveraged for supernatural breakthrough. In that sense, honor "weaponizes," and it becomes, through God, a catalyst for victory.

* * *

Before we see honor in action, we must establish some definitions and lay out some immutable principles. We must also set forth the following truth and lay hold of it throughout

INTRODUCTION

the remainder of this book. When love is expressed though honor towards our enemies, it becomes a weapon through which God executes justice and vengeance on our behalf. However, we must never carry honor with the intent of seeing our enemies taken out. Our agenda must always be redemption and reconciliation. Even when our most bitter enemies are being dealt with by God, due to unrepentant hearts, our stance must be that of compassion and forgiveness. We were not sent to this earth by YHVH as agents of judgment and punishment; rather, we were sent as dispensers of hope and love: *"vessels for honor, sanctified and useful to the master, prepared for every good work"* (2 Timothy 2:21).

Chapter 1

Honor as a Verb

Honor is high regard or respect that is given primarily for accomplishment, status, the value others place on us, and the inheritance we leave behind. Let's explore this definition, this use of *honor* as noun, with David in mind. In the biblical narrative, we first meet David as a boy. Samuel had gone to David's father's house to anoint the next king. Jesse called in all his sons, all except David. He was not a full brother to the others. Even by David's own admission in one of his songs, he was *"brought forth in iniquity, and in sin [his] mother conceived [him]"* (Psalms 51:5). As the product of an illegitimate affair between Jesse and David's mother, David held no honor in his household. He was not valued. He had no achievements on his record. He held no position except as shepherd over Jesse's flock. He had nothing by way of inheritance or legacy. David was not considered as a candidate for the throne. But none of Jesse's seven sons presented to Samuel who seemed suitable were selected by God to be king. Samuel asked Jesse if perhaps there was another son. "Sure... there's one more," Jesse must have said hesitantly. "He's out with the sheep."

Within minutes, David was brought forth and declared

the next king. Was there any honor given to David after that encounter? No. He was unceremoniously sent back with the sheep while the brothers went on to bigger assignments, such as fighting the Philistines in the Valley of Elam with King Saul and his army. Yet, at that very battlefield things would take a dramatic turn for David.

Note that David remained faithful to assignments from his earthly father. He watched over flocks of sheep, brought supplies to the battlefield, and returned with updates from the front lines. All the tasks were mundane, without any glory or influence connected to them. That is, they were without any glory connected to them on earth.

In Heaven, however, faithfulness with tedious, daily tasks, as well as with properly aligning ourselves with our earthy parents' wishes, carries much weight. In other words, by being obedient to Jesse and the menial things he assigned, David was demonstrating the values his Heavenly Father and all of Heaven were looking for, thus positioning himself in the center of God's will for his life.

David's identity and character were forged in Heaven, in the realms he had learned to navigate through wholehearted worship and devotion. Then, out of that heavenly reality from which he was living, David would function on earth, demonstrating the godly attributes and the heavenly deposits that had been made in his life. When David told King Saul that God had helped him prevail over the lion and the bear that had attacked his sheep, he was referring to the supernatural strength and courage he had found through relationship with YHVH.

From Heaven First

The same concept played out in terms of honor, because honor came to David from Heaven first—when the Father Himself declared He had found in David, a man after His own heart. Then circumstances on earth would line up for David to take his stand and show the world who he really was. Honor from men would follow. Our key is to recognize that David lived and operated from heavenly places towards this world, instead of trying to touch Heaven from the earth.

Many people have the sequence inverted. They seek the honor that comes from men, without properly qualifying for it first in Heaven. Even if men do bestow honor on us, it does not carry lasting impact without Heaven's assent.

Let's continue looking at the scene that unfolded in King David's tent shortly after Goliath's demise.

Then as David returned from the slaughter of the Philistine, Abner took him and brought him before Saul with the head of the Philistine in his hand (1 Samuel 17:57).

That is one picture I wish somebody had taken so I could enlarge, frame, and put it on my wall: David in the tent, holding the head of Goliath without saying a word. *No comment*, reads the caption. In the background, we would see the king and all the people who told David, "You cannot do it; you should not do it," or, "Here, use my armor to do it."

Sometimes we need to simply walk in with the proof of victory and not speak at all. Let the fruit of your life—the fruit that remains—speak for who you are and what you are capable of. Demonstrate what God can do through you when you are properly aligned with Him in devotion, obedience, and surrender to His will.

Honor Comes to David

When David walked in with the head of Goliath, for the first time in his life, honor began to come to him—it was honor for his achievement. People will first value achievement and position, but God always looks at our value and legacy.

David, standing there with the head of Goliath, had Saul's full attention. Saul asked, "Whose son are you?" That simple question represents honor coming from the king. He specifically wanted to know, "What generational line did you come through to be able to do this great thing today?" His question implies David's accomplishment must stem from a lineage of greatness, so asking, "Whose son are you?" was a way in which Saul was bestowing a degree of honor. Then Saul made David the captain of his guard, over the very people who told him, "You cannot do this," including his brothers, who ended up having to take orders from him. I would love to see the video of them announcing, "Hey, guys! We have a new commander: it is your brother David!" Women would even write a song to commemorate David, *"Saul has slain his thousands, And David his ten thousands"* (1 Samuel 18:7). That is honor for achievement!

David had such *"integrity of his heart"* and *"skillfulness of his hands"* (Psalms 78:72) that he did all things well and the people noticed. They began to honor him not only for his achievements, but also for his worth. In that army, he was becoming valuable. Even Saul recognized his value. Now, David was honored for his achievement and he was honored for his worth to the army, but God had told David through Samuel that he would have a position. Through that position David would obtain the honor he would leverage to establish the kind of platform that would ultimately bring him the honor he yearned for most—the honor associated with inheritance and legacy.

It was all connected. He killed the giant, he led the army, he did everything well. Then, he started dodging the jealous king's spears. As terrible as that season of persecution must have been for David, I strongly believe it was a prescribed and beneficial process that ultimately transformed David from shepherd to king. The character David developed during his years on the run from Saul played a huge role in David's longevity and success as Israel's king. I am not suggesting that Saul's attacks were God-initiated or sanctioned; rather that YHVH, *"who works all things for good for those who love him and are called according to his purpose"* (Romans 8:28), worked persecution to David's advantage. Integrity of heart comes from the process of character development, most of which is painful. The spotlight that shines on us on life's platforms never shines on the rocky paths we must first traverse to get there. As someone once said, "Champions are not made in the ring, they are only recognized there." Champions are made in the gym where nobody is watching and no one is there to cheer.

Exchanging Worldly for Heavenly Alliances

When something or someone bothers you and is a thorn in your flesh, consider not employing rebukes as your first response. Trust God and submit fully to Him and to His plans for your life. *"Therefore submit to God. Resist the devil and he will flee from you"* (James 4:7). Let God bring you through that process while spears are coming at you, while you are dwelling in caves, while you're facing all manner of trial. Let Him apply His grace to your hardship so He can transform you from what you were into who He destined you to become.

Jesus said to his disciples, *"Follow me and I will make you fishers of men"* (Matthew 4:19). They were not fishers of men to begin with, but in the process of being with Him, they would become something they could not have imagined being. I believe it was just as supernatural for them not to catch fish as it was for them to catch many fish the next day. Sometimes God wants you to be in a place where you catch nothing, so you can listen to the One who is not even a fisherman telling you what to do. Because beyond the catch itself is the process of becoming, and that is more important to God.

When David becomes king, he is honored for his position. All the people came to him for his worth. Even to the very end when he was fighting against Absalom, his own son, and desired to lead the armies to battle, David's officers did not allow him to do so. They said something to this effect: "You cannot go, we cannot spare you, you are still the best warrior." So except for killing Goliath, David has not experienced the honor people give for achievement, position and worth; however, David was willing to trade those forms of honor by the way he lived and administered the kingdom he was entrusted with, to establish lasting honor—honor for legacy. David was more interested in seeing Solomon go further and accomplish more than he was in cashing in on all the benefits his position of honor could offer.

Many leaders mistake receiving huge bonuses, benefits and awards as the highest form of honor. Leaders in the church and leaders in the marketplace—we are really guilty for this—accepting bonuses, planes, Ski-doos, Sea-doos, Lamborghinis, and all such perks. We think it is about us. We think that is all honor is. We think we deserve it. "Finally, they are paying their dues after I paid mine." No! We must be willing to trade material benefits or prestige in order to reach a higher platform, where we can obtain greater things to lay down before God. It has to be leveraged; it has to be traded. We must be willing to sacrifice everything all over again. That is what establishes lasting increase.

David understood this principle and would not rest on his laurels. He was not impressed with what people thought about him. He was not persuaded by his own advertising. David did not promote himself, but continued to walk in humility and press in for more. Did he make mistakes? Yes. Did he sin against the holiness of God? Yes, but God forgave him. The whole time He was preparing another king, one who came from David's own loins and would lead Israel to a higher place.

The kingdom was never meant to diminish, and it would not have if Solomon had not made bad alliances.

This point is crucial—we must make the right alliances Solomon allied with the wrong kings and married their daughters. I joke that Solomon married the wrong wives and thus inherited the wrong mothers-in-law. In marrying the wrong wives, Solomon dishonored God, because his wives turned his heart away from God. Solomon lost honor in Heaven, and in time that reality manifested in the kingdom of Israel through division and wars. Remember how David first obtained honor in Heaven and then honor came to him from people on earth? The opposite happened in Solomon's case. He chose the wrong associations on earth. He was seduced by counterfeit honor, the kind men exchange while making deals that Heaven hasn't endorsed. Solomon's associations caused him to lose credibility in Heaven; ultimately, they hurt him on earth as well. We cannot establish kingdoms that operate "on earth as it is in Heaven" unless we build and operate earthly kingdoms on Heaven's terms.

Honor: The Verb vs. the Noun

Now that we have explored the definition for honor through David's life, let us consider another foundational concept that we are examining in this book. In God's Kingdom, honor must operate in verb form more than it does as a noun. *Honor*, as we see it on a daily basis in the world, is mostly referred to as a noun, defined as a person, place, thing or idea. Honor is an idea, a concept, thus it is a noun. In describing the honor that came to David at various stages of his life, we were examining *honor* in that sense, as a noun, as the concept. To further understand and properly operate in the concept of honor, we must engage with *honor* as a verb, an action verb to be exact. For example, "They decided to honor the woman with a plaque." That means they chose to bestow honor on a woman by doing something for her—buying or preparing a plaque. That is when honor is activated—when it operates in our lives as an action verb; when we *do* something to express the honor that we feel toward someone.

In 1990, while in my dorm room at a college campus in New Jersey, I had a most-significant encounter with YHVH the God of the Bible. He appeared to me in a dream and lovingly called me into relationship with Him and to His service. Shortly after that encounter, God orchestrated events which brought me into relationship with Pastor Ron Bradley and the church family he was leading at the time. Pastor Bradley showed great interest in me and took precious time from his busy schedule to disciple me. For more than three years, he taught me about God, His love, His word, His ways. I consider Pastor Bradley my spiritual father. I have the deepest sense of honor in my heart for him. But unless I take action and do something to demonstrate that sense of honor, honor remains a noun—a mere feeling, a prompting, a state of the heart.

Though many things have changed in both our lives, and distance and time impacted my communication with Pastor Bradley, I never forgot what he did for me. When I started writing and publishing books in 2009, I decided to activate honor—to shift from *honor:* noun to *honor:* action verb. I designated a percentage of all profit from my first book, and all upcoming books, to Pastor Bradley and his family. To this day, though we talk infrequently, but the relationship between us is strong. Honor is setting a precedent and is making a strong statement generationally. The concept is so crucial that it is repeated in both the Old and New Testaments: *"Honor your father and mother...that it may be well with you..."* (Ephesians 6:3 taken from Exodus 20:12). Honor has to materialize. It has to translate into action.

That honor must be activated is an important concept to keep in mind if we consider the story of Esther. The stakes for her were high, perhaps as high as they can ever get. Esther's life was on the line, as were the lives of all of God's people, the Jews living in the Persian kingdom. A decree had already been signed—a death warrant—through which all Jews would be exterminated on a specific day. That day was approaching.

God is not mentioned once in the book of Esther, but he is not absent from the picture. His love was present, in the form of honor. Honor: the verb. Honor: the action. Honor, the intervention. Honor: the catalyst for breakthrough and the deliverance of God's people. Honor: the vehicle through which God executed justice and vengeance on behalf of Esther and the Jews. Honor kept a low profile in the land, until it was time to be wielded as an integral part of YHVH's strategy—to be deployed as a tactical weapon from Heaven.

CHAPTER 2

BEST LAID PLANS

I would like us to take a journey together through time and space to Shushan, the kingdom of King Ahasuerus (also believed to be Xerxes) during the height of the Persian Empire, circa 480 B.C. We do not know exactly how the scene played out, but there is good reason to envision it as follows.

It is late at night. With the exception of the guards stationed at various points, the king's courts are vacated. Oil lamps are burning, casting a soft glow against the palace walls. The faint sound of dogs howling echoes in the distance. The city is sleeping, as are all the king's courtiers and confidants—except one. He walks from his own house to the palace at a quick pace, his robe fluttering in the soft breeze. He makes no eye contact with anyone, even the king's guards. He approaches the outer court of the king's quarters and his gaze remains fixed on the doors he is about to burst through. His name: Haman. He is filled with hatred—no, with genocidal rage. He despises the Jews and wants them annihilated, particularly a man named Mordecai. This Jew has refused to bow to Haman when he walks by as Shushan's citizens are obligated to do.

Haman has already managed to convince the king to sign a decree ordering all the Jews to be killed on the thirteenth day of the twelfth month, the month of Adar. It cost Haman quite a bit to accomplish this—an offering of ten thousand silver talents into the king's treasury, to be exact—but it is well worth it to Haman, so long as Mordecai dies along with the rest of the Jews.

But Mordecai's planned demise was not enough for Haman. He could not wait that long. Earlier that very day, while Haman was returning home from a banquet Queen Esther had held to honor him and King Ahasuerus, he saw Mordecai sitting by the king's gate. Once again, Mordecai refused to pay homage to Haman. The Bible says, *"When Haman saw Mordecai in the king's gate, and that he did not stand or tremble before him, he was filled with indignation against Mordecai"* (Esther 5:9).

Even so, Haman *"restrained himself and went home, and he sent and called for his friends and his wife Zeresh"* (Esther 5:10). He proceeded to give himself the respect that had been withheld from him by Mordecai. A bragging session ensued, during which *"Haman told them of his great riches, the multitude of his children, everything in which the king had promoted him, and how he had advanced him above the officials and servants of the king"* (Esther 5:11). He then spoke of the banquet Queen Esther had invited him to earlier that day and of the upcoming encore banquet that she was preparing for the very next day.

The Havoc of Hatred

Talking about all his accomplishments and stature did not help Haman with his anger issue. When he got to the end of his self-promoting rant, he realized that *"All this avails me nothing, so long as I see Mordecai the Jew sitting at the king's gate"* (Esther 5:13). Seeing his frustration, Haman's company suggested a gallows be erected and that Haman petition the king to hang Mordecai immediately. No sooner had the words left his wife's mouth than Haman gave the order to build the gallows and stormed out of his house, making a beeline for the king's palace.

His mind was racing, and in that mind Haman had the details all sorted out. It should be easy to get the king's approval for the hanging. Having already manipulated Ahasuerus with the silver talents, the path for Haman getting his way had been well-paved. Mordecai's destruction was only minutes away. Haman picked up the pace to a near jog.

Hatred is a powerful force, one that has historically wreaked havoc on the earth by inciting wars, purges, mass executions, terrorism, and all manner of violence. And surely genocidal hatred was fast at work that night in Shushan. But unbeknown to Haman, another force, more powerful than Haman's rage, had been deployed. That force? Honor.

Yes, Haman was able to seduce Ahasuerus into signing the death warrant for all the Jews. Surely, Haman seemed to have the upper hand as he had won the king's favor. Yet from Heaven's perspective, Haman was as good as dead. He was outnumbered and outmaneuvered. He just did not know it yet, and by the time he found out, it would be too late. Racism and pride had blinded Haman, driving him step by step and stomp by stomp to his demise. That very day he would die on the same gallows he had erected for Mordecai. Honor had been making the arrangements for quite some time. Honor would hang the noose around Haman's neck. God would execute vengeance and His people would find justice.

A Sleepless Night

At the very moment Haman entered the inner court and was only steps away from the king's chambers, a different scenario was unfolding altogether: *"That night the king could not sleep. So one was commanded to bring the book of the records of the chronicles; and they were read before the king"* (Esther 6:1).

WEAPONIZED HONOR

I find it interesting that of all the things the sleepless king could have engaged with in the middle of his restless night, he chose to bring in someone to read the detailed record of days gone by from the kingdom's chronicles. At some point in the reading, the record indicated that a while back, the king's life had been saved by Mordecai when he uncovered a conspiracy against the monarch. Mordecai had alerted Queen Esther to the threat and she in turn warned the king's guard. The plotters had been apprehended and executed.

We do not know how much the king himself knew about the plot, but we do know that upon hearing the matter, Ahasuerus was uneasy. Perhaps he had been too preoccupied with the affairs of the kingdom so a plot such as this barely appeared on the king's radar. Or perhaps his courtiers handled the issue very discreetly, relegating the details to the chronicles instead of disclosing them in their morning briefing sessions with King Ahasuerus. Either way, when the records were read to him, the king felt that the case had not been properly closed. A very significant part was missing: there was no record of anything having been done to honor Mordecai for his intervention.

> *And it was found written that Mordecai had told of Bigthana and Teresh, two of the king's eunuchs, the doorkeepers who had sought to lay hands on King Ahasuerus. Then the king said, "What honor or dignity has been bestowed on Mordecai for this?*
>
> *And the king's servants who attended him said, "Nothing has been done for him"* (Esther 6:2-3).

Remember, honor cannot merely function in our lives as a warm fuzzy feeling—in noun form. It must also stir us to action. If simply feeling grateful was honorable, then honor would have been served. If simply writing about the incident in the book and keeping a record of it was honorable, honor would have been served. Yet, the king did not feel right because Mordecai had not been honored properly.

Awakened by Honor
It is my conviction that the king was awakened by Honor; not the noun or even the action verb form of honor, but a being from the heavenly realm, a courtier from God's courts—a servant of the Spirit of the Lord. If this description sounds too mystical and you struggle with the concept of any other heavenly beings beyond the Holy Trinity and guardian angels being intricately involved with our affairs in this world (I say this respectfully), then think of Honor as an angelic being. In the book of Proverbs, Solomon repeatedly refers to Wisdom using feminine pronouns. He speaks of a female entity with whom he interacts continually, not an ethereal force which makes good ideas pop into people's heads. Solomon encountered and engaged with Wisdom, a heavenly being who was with God from the beginning. *"In the beginning I was there, for God possessed me even before he created the universe"* (Proverbs 8:22 TPT). There is a spiritual dimension in which we, too, can encounter Honor.

I have been engaged with the person of Honor for several years, and I am convinced that I have been tutored by this being throughout my life. At some of the most critical moments, Honor has counseled me and has shown me the way to great breakthroughs. People ask me if I have seen Honor in the spirit realm. I have not. However, I know the difference between the honor that dwells *in* my heart and the influence of Honor—the being—*upon* my heart. I have also been asked if perhaps I am misinterpreting this presence as something extra-biblical, when it is really the Holy Spirit's presence that I feel. I must say that I have had many encounters with the person of the Holy Spirit, and from my experiences, I can confidently state that Honor and the Holy Spirit are not the same: not any more than my wife and mother are the same person.

It is important for me to state that all my encounters with heavenly beings, including Honor, are the product of my relationship with YHVH, and Yeshua is the Door through which I enter to engage with heavenly realms and beings. I do not encourage anyone to pursue a relationship with heavenly beings apart from an intimate, passionate walk with Jesus. Relationship with Him is paramount. Every other experience and interaction must stem from that primary relationship. I do not pursue spiritual encounters. I pursue Him, and other heavenly encounters come only from that pursuit.

People also ask me if I believe everyone is to pursue a relationship with the heavenly beings I speak about. My response is always that every individual must develop his/her own walk with YHVH. Out of that union with Him will come all the promptings and directives for engagements with heavenly beings.

Whether we perceive honor as only a concept or also as a being, one thing is certain: Honor will open more doors for us than education; it can promote us faster than any climb up the corporate ladder; it can protect us from the most well-laid plans against our lives. It did so for Mordecai. Honor kept the king awake that night in Shushan, because Haman was on his way to make a case for Mordecai's immediate execution. But Honor's intervention was not isolated to the events of that moment. It was part of a much bigger plan—a multi-faceted, heaven-run operation. The success of the operation hinged on several moving pieces coming together. Esther's part was huge. So was Mordecai's. We will return to each of them in more detail in later chapters. Honor also had a large part. For the operation against Haman to work, Honor, the heavenly being, had to find honor, the verb, in the king's heart and in the land.

Chapter 3

Kingdom of Honor

In the previous chapter, we encountered the Persian king Ahasuerus, who had a sleepless night at a very crucial moment for his kingdom. It was a moment when his chief prince, Haman—the man who had manipulated King Ahasuerus to sign a decree for the extermination of all the Jews—was about to petition the king to issue orders for Mordecai's immediate execution. But that outcome could not prevail that night. There was too much at stake from Heaven's side for Mordecai to die at Haman's hands.

Mordecai raised Esther, who had lost her mother and father. He had a significant part in the development of her character and spiritual upbringing. Furthermore, Mordecai looked out for Esther during the period of purification and beautification she underwent before spending her one night with the king. He hung around the gate to the palace and inquired of Esther's wellbeing continually. It is because of her lifelong relationship to Mordecai that Esther heeded his advice when he shared the news of Haman's plan against the Jews. Mordecai told Esther the bad news and asked her to go before the king to make an appeal for the lives of her people.

At first Esther hesitated, but Mordecai's "for such a time as this" speech convinced her to appear to make her appeal after a time of fasting and prayer (see Esther 4:13-14).

Mordecai's active role in the plan seems to have been completed when Esther agreed to give his recommendation a chance. It was not. Mordecai's presence and input in Esther's life was important to her. She needed his counsel and moral support. Have you ever wondered what would have happened to Esther if Mordecai had been hanged that night? Where would such news have left her? Esther was between two banquets she had committed to host. One had already taken place and the second was lined up for the next day. Esther was preparing for feasts and sitting across from the man who had unknowingly signed her death sentence and who had engineered the holocaust-in-the-making. Would she have had the nerve to carry on without Mordecai? If Haman had succeeded in hanging Mordecai, could Esther have kept her cool long enough during the second banquet to ask the king what she desired?

These are all questions for which we have no answers. However, they lead me to the conclusion that Haman could not have been allowed to win that night—Mordecai had to be saved.

Esther was already on track with her part of the operation—the plan which she received during her time of fasting and prayer. Honor had the other major part, and for that piece to work, Heaven would have to leverage the honor found in the king's life and in the realm he was governing.

So, I believe it was Honor, the heavenly being, who nudged the king awake. Honor stirred his heart to revisit the chronicles, because Honor found honor in this king and kingdom. It is as though Honor had been hovering over the land, waiting to be released into the kingdom.

I believe Honor will not leave those of us who carry honor

in our hearts alone until we do what is right by Honor. That the king asked what had been done to honor Mordecai is indicative of two realities. First, the king carried honor in himself—that is why he asked. Second, the Persian kingdom operated with protocols of honor in place. Think about this example: Esther, who was queen, had to risk her life to appear before the king uninvited. Why? The level of risk implies that it was considered extremely dishonorable for people to disturb the king and appear before his throne without a proper invitation. Also consider the practice of the king extending his golden scepter towards those he chose to spare. That is an honorable deed, stemming from mercy and grace. There are other examples, such as the former queen Vashti's refusal to dance and expose herself before her inebriated husband (the king) and his drunk friends. There were undoubtedly honor protocols in the land and in the king's behavior. Thus, at the moment the (honorable) king Ahasuerus inquired as to why his (honorable) government had not honored Mordecai, Honor found opportunity to make an entrance and save the day.

* * *

Let's go back to that night in Shushan. Here comes Haman knocking on the king's door. *"And the king said, 'Let him come in.' So Haman came in, and the king asked him. 'What shall be done for the man whom the king delights to honor?'"* (Esther 6:6). Haman's hatred and pride had so tainted his heart that he immediately assumed he was the one to be honored. Therefore, Haman advised the king according to his own personal desires.

And Haman answered the king, "For the man whom the king delights to honor, let a royal robe be brought which the king has worn, and a horse on which the king has ridden, which has a royal crest placed on its head. Then let this robe and horse be delivered to the hand of one of the king's most noble princes, that he may array the man whom the king delights to honor. Then parade him on horseback through the city square, and proclaim before him: 'Thus shall it be done to the man whom the king delights to honor!'" (Esther 6:7-9).

The next scene is beautiful. If only we could have a picture of Haman's face as the king issued his next order: The king said to Haman, *"Hurry, take the robe and the horse, as you have suggested, and do so for Mordecai the Jew"* (Esther 6:10). Can you feel the vibration of that? "For Mordecai the Jew." That picture! Picture, too, one of Haman parading Mordecai through the streets, loudly proclaiming: "The king honors this man!" Honor had orchestrated the sequence of events perfectly. And honor set the stage for Esther to execute her part of the mission.

* * *

Over the last few years, some outstanding works have been produced and have spread internationally on the subject of honor. From my deepest parts, I rejoice over all such contributions, and I give honor to the authors, filmmakers, conference speakers, and church leaders who have emphasized the importance of honor in our day. We need honor in our interpersonal communications, our relationships, and in all our dealings. Operating honorably certainly bears much fruit. Honor also sells well. It should. Books and teaching materials about the subject should indeed be produced and made available worldwide. But leaders cannot capitalize financially and make a name for themselves by piggy-backing on the platforms of those who have received revelation about honor and who genuinely apply these principles to their lives.

Moreover, honor cannot be reduced to a buzzword, the latest Christian cliché.

In every country I minister in, I hear leaders expressing the desire to establish "cultures of honor" in their organizations, be they businesses, ministries, even governmental bodies. The concept of operating within a culture of honor is appealing and it can be very beneficial. It is an excellent pursuit and I respect those who have presented honor through language that is easy to understand. I believe when honor is embraced and properly engaged, an honorable culture will certainly be established—not because we pay lip service to the principle, rather because the individuals involved carry honor in their hearts. That is where honor has to be established first. The heart is the place from which true cultures of honor originate. Our hearts must be aligned with God's heart. Our lives must be marked with the precepts that govern His kingdom. If God's values and standards are not operating inside of us first, any systems we try to build on various concepts will rest on faulty foundations.

I am shocked when I hear people invoking culture of honor terminology where jealousy, gossip, and bitterness are rampant among their communities, where control and manipulation operate through their platforms. If honor is nothing more than new, shiny packaging for authoritarian leadership, it will have little impact and it will not produce lasting fruit. On the flip side, it is wonderful to experience the blessings of honor among those who are genuine and pure in living out of that reality. Genuine, heartfelt, and life-tested honor is powerful. Even one individual with a heart of honor can bring change in spiritual atmospheres and can impact broader groups and larger spheres of influence.

A few years ago, six weeks before we were scheduled to host a major conference at our church, I received a message. My family and I were living in Cyprus at the time, and the messaged happened to come when I was on a flight to the U.S. It had been a rough season building up to this conference. Not many people had registered, several delegates had cancelled, and the church felt financially challenged. Morale was low even among my closest confidants. The message I received came from the Holy Spirit. He nudged me on that flight, saying, "Within a few hours from when you land, three different people are going to recommend you cancel the conference because there are not enough registrations." That was what I heard from the Spirit. I did not know any of the details. The plane landed and within two hours, three different people from our team approached me in the kindest way—trying to be good stewards and doing their job—saying, "It is not looking good, Marios. We have fourteen people signed up and we are a month and a half out."

I had already heard from the Lord what I was to do, so I said to them, "If I have to lose everything and have to flip burgers for the rest of my life to cover the costs, this conference will take place. We are not cancelling."

Nothing really changed until a week or so before the conference when the registrations got us to just about half of what we needed to meet the budget. (As a side note, our conference budgets are high because we insist on giving proper honor to our speakers and event staff.)

The day the conference was set to begin, a white SUV pulled into the parking lot. In the SUV was a friend of ours from Georgia, along with people serving her international ministry. The moment they arrived, there was an atmospheric shift in the spirit realm. The reason for that shift was these friends' thoughtfulness and generosity. They had prepared for weeks to honor us for hosting the conference. They got out of the vehicle and unloaded multiple bags of gifts. They piled beautifully wrapped presents in our office area. The first gift was a leather box with gold, frankincense, and myrrh.

There was a small treasure chest with gemstones. There were gifts for the speakers and their spouses; gifts for the church leaders; gifts for the staff.

We had an explosive start to the conference. Everything came together. There was powerful worship, revelatory teaching, and abundance of resources. God used the honor in these ladies' hearts to change the tide of that conference and to facilitate the needed financial support. Because her heart was filled with honor—both *honor* the noun and *honor* the action—there was a breakthrough anointing on our friend to shift the atmosphere. While they may not have been the givers of the largest monetary sums (atmosphere changers do not have to be), they set things in place spiritually to activate a spirit of generosity and financial freedom in the whole conference community. The honor in our friend's heart connected and arced with the honor in the church, and then it exploded in a way that benefitted everyone who attended.

* * *

Going back to David's story for a moment, let's examine how honor in David's heart and in his camp made an impact on the warfront.

While the Philistine garrison was in Bethlehem, David was with his mighty men outside the city. It had been prophesied, *"But you, Bethlehem… though you are little… yet out of you shall come forth to Me the One to be Ruler in Israel"* (Micah 5:2). The Philistines were occupying the town, and at the moment it did not look as though anything was going to come out of Bethlehem. David was encamped with his men nearby and he said, *"… Oh, that someone would give me a drink of water from the well of Bethlehem, which is by the gate!"* (1 Chronicles 11:17).

Perhaps David and his men were sitting around a fire sharing stories when David expressed his longing for

Bethlehem water. Maybe the guy who killed eight hundred in one confrontation was sitting next to the guy who killed the lion in its own pit on a snowy day, and the guy whose sword cleaved to his hand because he fought so hard. They may have all been around the fire. When David spoke, I believe they looked at each other with the expression, "Did you hear what the king said? He wants water from Bethlehem. We are doing this tonight!" Maybe it was just a look. Sometimes, a look is all you need. They were trained to engage assignments with just one look.

Three mighty men went, broke through the Philistine's camp, got the water, and brought it back. When the men presented the water to David, he refused to drink it. Recognizing that his men had risked their lives to obtain the water, David chose to pour the water on the ground as an offering to the Lord. Honor was operating on different levels in this episode. The men honored David; David honored his men; David honored God with something natural that had much value ascribed to it by this point.

David established a culture of honor among his men from the time they were in caves. The kingdom of honor that he established in a cave set in place the protocol which allowed him to expand honor's reach when it was time: out of a cave, into a palace, and into a kingdom that would change everything. David poured the water out unto the Lord on the ground. When the water hit the ground, the vibrational frequency of the land recognized where that water came from and what trading platform it was being traded on. The land knew who it wanted to be ruled by and it was not the Philistines! What I am saying is that the land repelled the ones that did not belong there. David did not have to fight them at that time because the sons of God walked the earth in their destiny. They manifested the Kingdom of God and walked that level of honor and high trading in such a way that it changed the frequency of the land. The ruler of that land was standing on it and therefore the Philistines had to go, because Bethlehem had a destiny greater than any the Philistines could ever bring there. Yeshua would come through Bethlehem.

Instead of competing to show ourselves greater or more correct in our doctrine than others, we must recognize and then start from a place of humble honor. Honor and the way we value each other in the Kingdom is paramount.

Chapter 4

Woman: God's Secret Weapon

Haman's plot was near perfect. He had thought of every angle and had covered all the bases: Grease my way to a promotion as prince? *Check.* Manipulate the king through a sizeable donation to his treasury fund? *Check.* Fabricate accusations against the Jews to secure a royal decree for their extermination? *Check.* Become rich? *Check.* Become powerful? *Check.* Become influential? *Check.*

Moreover, Queen Esther herself had recently made an appearance in court, after a rather long absence from royal circles. "Who knows why," Haman thought. "The king's preferences of women keep shifting, plus he's been so busy lately. But who cares?" On the day that Queen Esther walked into court and stood before the golden scepter Ahasuerus favorably extended towards her, she asked for just one thing: "Would the king and Haman attend a banquet she was hosting in their honor?"

Everything had worked so well for Haman. Life was good. Well, all but the slight hiccup of the previous night—that nasty business of having to lead the king's horse around town with Mordecai in the saddle. It was the hardest thing he had ever had to do, no doubt: and he was still very upset about the incident. "*...Haman hurried home utterly humiliated*" (Esther 6:12 TLB). He had undoubtedly suffered a blow, but then he thought of the bigger picture. At least his idea of how to honor Mordecai had drawn accolades from the king. "Brilliant idea, Haman! You came in at the ideal moment, and I surely appreciate you. Great having you around!"

Haman could not get bogged down with the fact that Mordecai had been honored instead of hanged. The Jews would all be killed soon, and Mordecai would perish with them—the plan was still very much in effect. Keep the king happy and everything works out in the end. Plus, come evening time, he and Ahasuerus would be together again, reclining at Esther's table. "Maybe the queen has taken a liking to me," he thought as he entered the courtyard to his own house, "professional in nature, of course. But who knows where things can lead? After all, I am the only other person she chose to invite—not just to one banquet, but now to a second one." Deep in thought, Haman walked into the house and lay down on a sofa.

"How did it go?" Zeresh asked. "Heard a rumor you were parading Mordecai through the streets, shouting that he was the man the king wants to honor. I'm starting to get concerned for us. I sent for some of our friends. Let's talk this through."

Esther was Haman's greatest miscalculation. Whether he entertained thoughts similar to those in my embellished account above or not, one thing is certain: Haman never saw Esther coming—he was completely blindsided. At the same time, Esther was Heaven's greatest asset in Persia. She had been prepared for this assignment throughout her entire life. God found in Esther the character qualities needed for the critical mission in Shushan, circa 480 B.C.

WOMAN: GOD'S SECRET WEAPON

* * *

I was born with a defect on my face that covered half of one side. To date, I have had fifteen rounds of laser surgery which has removed most of it. From the time of my birth until my mid-thirties, whenever I walked into a room, the first thing people noticed was my birthmark.

Greek culture has a superstitious mindset about blemishes—that those who bear them are marked by God. Jesus was asked this question, *"...Rabbi, who sinned, this man or his parents, that he was born blind?"* (John 9:2). Similar thinking prevailed in Cyprus while I was growing up. The blemish itself and the cultural mindsets about such matters rendered me unable to have romantic relationships during my teenage years. My interactions with female classmates and other girls in my adolescent orbit were limited to friendship. As my kids say, I was forever "friend-zoned." Once when I asked a friend to an upcoming dance, she did not talk to me for three months, because I had the audacity to imagine I could take her out on a date!

Even though I had the mark, I was gifted with a dynamic leadership personality. I was involved with student government and sports, and those activities opened many doors for friendship with girls. And because both they and their parents were certain that the friendship would never progress beyond the platonic level, girls trusted me. They asked for advice and shared their deepest secrets, including the guys they liked (instead of me, of course).

When I spent time with my female classmates, fellow athletes, or girls from the neighborhood, the thought of ever being together was off the table from the start. Therefore, I learned to value girls for who they were on the inside. By default—not because I consciously chose this course—I developed a respect for women during the season when most boys focus primarily on girls' sex appeal. I realized that women are amazing and I have been growing in that understanding ever since.

During a conference in Singapore, my friend Ian Clayton taught about Man and Woman in their First Estate—the time when they lived in harmony with God and one another before the fall. Through his teaching, I recognized that men and women were created and empowered by God to rule over everything else God had created, and that they are to do this together. They are to be co-rulers of the universe, exercising dominion through their unique expressions, dispositions, and capabilities.

The Constraining Effects of Misconceptions of *Woman*
When we do not understand the First Estate Woman, it comes at the expense of women's assignment and capability to exercise authority—and it limits us all in relationships. Throughout our Christian lives we are told to avoid the appearance of evil. In my preparation for ministry, I heard it countless times: "Guard yourself from lust; do not talk to women alone; make sure you keep your door cracked open when you are counseling a woman." With such a mindset, fear and mistrust of ourselves and members of the opposite sex become the foundation for relationships, instead of the pure love and spirit of brotherhood that can and should characterize the interactions between men and women.

There is solid biblical reason why true sons should not have to keep doors cracked and utilize all sorts of disclaimers when interacting with women: *"To the pure all things are pure"* (Titus 1:15). In my experience, emphasis on avoiding the appearance of evil has always been at the expense of modeling the appearance of good. I can sit with one of my sisters and talk to her for hours without a thought of impropriety ever entering our minds. Why do we fear sin and magnify the enemy's workings to destroy lives? Why do we always revert to a defensive posture instead of engaging with the greater reality—that our pure interactions and relationships can provoke the world to a desire for Kingdom standards? People are looking for an example, a model of what is good and upright, and we have a chance to display it. Those who keep the door cracked when meeting with someone of the opposite sex (unless the guest requests this level of accountability) are not effectively dealing with the issue of lust if they have it, since they could very well be full of lust both before, during, and after the meeting. A cracked door solves nothing. Maybe the counselling in question needs to be conducted by a leader of the same sex.

More often than not, leaders who most emphasize the avoidance of the appearance of evil are the ones with the problem. During my early years in ministry, one particular ecclesiastical movement warned incessantly against pornography. The Internet was up and running and porn was fast becoming a big, ugly, readily-accessible vice. Over the years, it has become apparent that those preaching the fieriest anti-pornography sermons struggled with porn themselves. The issue of pornography was not even on my radar at the time. I was young, newly married, and not at all interested in fake, studio-scripted erotic stimulation. I can honestly say I have never visited a porn site on the Internet. I share this not to pat myself on the back—after all, the Bible clearly states, *"Therefore let him who thinks he stands take heed lest he fall"* (1 Corinthians 10:12). I also understand from Proverbs 7 that even the strongest of individuals can fail if they let their guard down in the face of potential seduction. I am very aware of that and I do not let my guard down. At the same time, I refuse to allow the fear of failure to spin me out of sonship and the ability to walk with women the way we have been destined to walk.

If church leaders have lust issues, they should go before YHVH and let Him purify their hearts so they feel free to interact with men/women as sons—in purity. But they should not try to make up for their own flaws by superimposing their issues over everyone else through erroneous teachings and wrong interpretations of Scripture.

One more point here: it is all about how men perceive women. If you are in fear of your responses because there is a woman present, then you are possibly misperceiving women. If you live in fear that your behavior will be inappropriate when you are with a woman, then it is likely that at least at partial fault is your misperception of the role and power God has created in women. Instead of fearing lust and sexual sin, and thereby taking a defensive posture in relationships, men need to view women as 'Woman' in her First Estate and that will certainly change things. Our misperceptions of women can wrongly influence our interpretations of Scripture. Proverbs 31:11 is often mistakenly interpreted as speaking of marital fidelity: *"The heart of her husband safely trusts her; So he will have no lack of gain."* Unfortunately, corrupted minds always go there, and I have heard it more times than I care to remember—"He trusts her not to cheat on him." Wrong. I do not believe trust here has to do with fidelity. Rather, it addresses Woman's ability and capacity to rule with Man. The wise wife's husband safely trusts her to exercise dominion with him the way God intended for Man and Woman to co-labor from the beginning. When Scripture says, *"the heart of her husband safely trusts her"* the whole idea of infidelity is not even on the table because this is Woman, encouraged by her husband and empowered by God to rule.

After the conference I mentioned above, I reflected more on Ian Clayton's description of Woman in her First Estate. I searched the Scriptures for examples of women who demonstrated both freedom and empowerment from their husbands and society to rule. The virtuous woman of Proverbs 31 is one such example. Another outstanding woman who models First Estate qualities is Esther. I will examine the wise wife closely and show how Queen Esther is like her.

The Wise Wife and Esther
The wise wife presented in the last chapter of Proverbs is not a specific woman. She is a woman in the First Estate—before Adam and Eve's fall in the garden of Eden. It is my conviction that given the opportunity to thrive within an empowering environment, every woman has the capacity to live in the standard set by the wise wife. Esther's preparation period, both while in Mordecai's care when she was young and later by the palace eunuchs responsible for the beautification of the potential queen, brought forth similar character qualities to those of the wise wife.

The description of the wise wife begins with a question: *"Who can find a virtuous wife? For her worth is far above rubies"* (Proverbs Proverbs 31:10). An individual who makes a statement like this must have had a virtuous wife *and* rubies I cannot tell you if something is worth more to me than rubies, when I have not actually owned rubies King Lemuel seems to have had both because he says, "her worth" is better and greater than rubies. Solomon says essentially the same thing about Wisdom in Proverbs: *"For her proceeds are better than the profits of silver, And her gain than fine gold"* (Proverbs 3:14). I point out the preeminence of the wise wife over rubies because her virtue, high as it is, is attainable. We are not discussing an ideal that cannot be reached.

In my recent book, *Sexy Laundry*, I explore the idea that the human race has not maximized its potential because, as a species, we have never fully valued and honored women. I draw from the description of the virtuous woman of Proverbs 31, whom I call *31w* or *the wise wife*, to present Woman as a powerful creation, destined to co-labor with Man, not merely act as his underling or sidekick. Woman is Man's equal in the spirit, both in her authority and ability to govern and to exercise dominion on the earth. In *Sexy Laundry*, I present the activities and character qualities of the wise wife in detail.

Let's consider them, taken here from The Passion Translation of Proverbs 31. The wise wife is:

Creative & Productive	*She searches out continually to possess that which is pure and righteous. She delights in the work of her hands (v. 13).*
A Divinely Inspired Leader	*She gives out revelation-truth to feed others. She is like a trading ship bringing divine supplies from the merchant (v. 14).*
An Excellent Housekeeper & Employer	*Even in the night season she arises and sets food on the table for hungry ones in her house and for others (v. 15).*
An Influencer in International Affairs	*She sets her heart upon a nation and takes it as her own, carrying it within her… (v. 16).*
An Entrepreneur	*…She labors there to plant the living vines (v. 16).*
Physically Fit	*She wraps herself in strength, might, and power in all her works (v. 17).*
Self-Confident	*…Her shining light will not be extinguished, no matter how dark the night (v. 18).*
A Co-Ruler	*She stretches out her hands to help the needy and she lays hold of the wheels of government (vv. 19-20).*
Benevolent	*She is known by her extravagant generosity to the poor, for she always reaches out her hands to those in need (v. 20).*
A Provider	*She is not afraid of tribulation, for all her household is covered in the dual garments of righteousness and grace (v. 21).*
Innovative & Creative	*Her clothing is beautifully knit together—purple gown of exquisite linen (v. 22).*
Supportive	*Her husband is famous and admired by all, sitting as the venerable judge of his people (v. 23).*

One Who Weaponizes Honor	*Even her works of righteousness she does for the benefit of her enemies (v. 24).*
Secure	*Bold power and glorious majesty are wrapped around her as she laughs with joy over the latter days (v. 25).*

All the wise wife's outstanding traits stem from honor and lead to honor. When Woman is operating in the fullness of God's blessing and empowerment, she is honoring towards everyone around her, and ultimately, she will be honored throughout her lifetime and for posterity.

God works with what we have on the inside. Our encounters and assignments stem from our unique physical, emotional, and spiritual makeup. Heaven gave Esther the strategy of honoring Haman to take him down, because Esther carried honor inside her. According to the plan, she had to "trade" honor to get Haman off guard, and Esther could not possibly trade something that was not a part of her—and would never have tried to—not when the stakes were so high and her very life was on the line. Someone other than Esther could have received a different strategy based on what they carried. Esther was honoring and honorable in all her ways—just like the wise wife—therefore she was directed to leverage honor in her mission against Haman.

'Woman' properly identified in her first estate is important to both how men perceive and co-rule with women, and important to how women conceive of their own identity and role in the Kingdom.

Chapter 5

Painting Targets

We had been in the same position for several hours: a handful of men, blending perfectly into the landscape, limiting our movement to the necessary expansion and contraction of our thoracic cavities for breathing. We began our movement at nightfall, crawling on our elbows and knees at first. Approaching the tower, we advanced slowly, using only hands and toes to shift our bodies forward. Then—the long wait in absolute silence. Central Command had briefed us extensively about the possibility of encountering enemy patrols, hence, the meticulous attention to detail requiring applications of camouflage, stealth in our movements, and stillness near the target.

It was approaching midnight when we heard the unmistakable sound of a jeep's engine and the rumble of the tires against the rough terrain. Though still far away, headlights swept over us and remained fixed on our position as the jeep approached.

"Stay down and don't move an inch," came the order in a loud whisper. It was from our captain, lying a few yards to our right. Nothing else was spoken. There was no need for clarification or further instruction. We knew the stakes and we understood our position. Every one of us knew exactly what to do in a situation like this—absolutely nothing.

I was serving my second year in the Cypriot Special Forces as a sniper. I had been selected to join a small team that would penetrate enemy lines and destroy a communications tower. We had arrived in the area a few days earlier and had set up camp a few miles south of our enemy's fortifications. We were operating on viable leads from our intelligence network as well as the steady flow of information from reconnaissance teams. We laid low during the day and mobilized at night, exploring routes of approach and demolitions methods. On that particular morning, word had come that the conditions were ideal for a takedown of the tower.

We were only about one hundred yards from the target, when the jeep we had heard moments earlier came to a stop just a few feet from some of our comrades. Two men got out and started walking towards us, weapons drawn. It seemed as if they knew exactly where to find us. Perhaps a tower guard had spotted us and called it in; or, using satellite technology, the enemy had been onto us from the moment we had left our camp.

As the jeep approached, I managed to turn around so I could face the vehicle if it came closer. Once the men disembarked, I set my sights on the man closest to me and followed his movements. Another sniper was undoubtedly locked onto the other passenger. The men spoke softly. From my night vision scope, I saw them searching the ground before them. One of them was surveying the area through night vision binoculars. I heard more talk in soft tones, then a crackle from one of the men's radios. I couldn't quite make out what was said, but I heard the soldier's response loud and clear.

"Nothing here; we're heading back."

A few hours later, in the relative safety and (minimal) comfort of our makeshift barracks, it became known that:

PAINTING TARGETS

- *Our mission was suspenseful: one of the two jeep passengers almost stepped on one of our men during their search for us in that field.*
- *Our mission was successful: we managed to remain undetected in our approach and we did indeed blow up the enemy's communication tower (it exploded in a huge ball of flames shortly after 1:00 a.m.).*
- *Our mission was unnecessary: at least the last part of it was.*

The entire operation had been a drill—a thoroughly planned and well-executed military drill, involving several branches of the armed forces. We were the tip of the spear, so to speak, and our efforts were the culmination of a multi-faceted preparation process. The "enemy" was comprised of officers from several Special Operations units. The "tower" was a wooden structure that had been erected by civilian contractors and installed on top of a hill days earlier.

Our mission was not deemed unnecessary because the whole op was a drill; rather, it was unnecessary because at the same time my team was stealthily moving towards the target from one direction, unbeknown to us, another group of commandos was approaching the same target from the other side. Their mission was very different than ours.

A much smaller contingent of men moved in on the tower until they were in position to point a laser beam at it. That was it. That was their objective—get close enough to point a laser at the target. The radiation bouncing off the target would then guide a remotely-launched missile (ground or air) straight to the tower. The technique is sometimes called semi-active radar homing (SARH) or semi-active laser homing (SALH). We simply referred to it as *painting the target*.

A missile was not launched against the tower that night due to economic and tactical considerations. The Cypriot armed forces did not want to incur the cost of such a missile launch. Nevertheless, the Green Berets got good training out of it on both sides of the operational spectrum. But one thing was made clear that night and it has stayed with me ever since: It is much easier to paint the target than to engage with it up close.

* * *

Let's switch now from the modern battlefield to ancient history. The stakes are much higher than those in a military training drill, but the tactics are very much the same as described above. Watch with me as Queen Esther paces in her room on the third day of her fast. We don't know exactly how God instructed her to proceed with making her petition before the king. But we do know what the strategy entailed—honor. The plan God gave Esther when she fasted coincided with what was already in the kingdom. Proceed and act with honor, as honor would provide the perfect cover.

As we saw earlier, the king was an honorable man—Heaven knew he would agree to attend the banquet and thus receive honor from his queen. Heaven had Haman figured out as well. A direct accusation against Haman before the king would not stick—not if Esther pulled that card on Haman's playing field. He had to be lured off base to a place where his guard would be down and he wouldn't be controlling the variables. Haman had exploitable weaknesses, the largest of which was his love for recognition—the more public and grandiose, the better. And everyone in the king's court heard Queen Esther's banquet invitation. Heaven knew Haman would filter the invitation through his pride-filled heart; thus, he would fall for the rouse, being none the wiser about what was really at work behind the scenes.

Heaven gave Esther a strategy by which honor would be the tip of her spear. Haman would be too preoccupied with his own thoughts of what the invitations meant and how great they made him look. He would not realize that the honor Esther was feigning was of the deadliest variety as it pertained to the enemies of God's people. Esther's honor was weaponized honor. In honor of Haman, wine was poured out and dishes were served. And through Honor's well-executed plot, a noose was being placed around Haman's neck. Esther chose honor as the means to expose and dismantle Haman's plot. When she did, Honor painted the target.

Before going further, it is important to note that Haman had an opportunity to repent by recognizing that he should have never put Mordecai or the Jews in his crosshairs. Those closest to Haman counselled him to abort his mission.

> *When Haman told his wife Zeresh and all his friends everything that had happened to him, his wise men and his wife Zeresh said to him, "If Mordecai, before whom you have begun to fall, is of Jewish descent, you will not prevail against him but will surely fall before him."* (Esther 6:13).

The reason this fact must be stated is because I want to emphasize once again that Heaven's first objective, even for the most vicious enemies of God, is redemption. In the Special Forces, we painted targets to destroy them. Heaven paints targets primarily to save them. If individuals like Haman choose to continue to veer off course, they will eventually face the consequences.

Esther served the meal and stood before her satisfied husband and king. He was intrigued by the mystery surrounding her appearance in his court. *"What is your petition Queen Esther? It shall be granted you. And what is your request, up to half the kingdom? It shall be done!"* (Esther 7:2). Without hesitation Esther asked for her life and for that of her people. *"For we have been sold, my people and I, to be destroyed, to be killed, and to be annihilated"* (Esther 7:4). The king was infuriated at the very notion that someone would dare lift a finger against his queen. *"Who is he, and where is he, who would dare presume in his heart to do such a thing?"* (Esther 7:5). Missiles fired. Haman's miserable life was within minutes from its bitter end.

Esther's face shifted from that of a gracious, honoring host, to a leader full of authority and power. She pointed her finger in Haman's direction and said, *"The adversary and enemy is this wicked Haman!"* (Esther 7:6). At those words, all of Heaven saw a ball of fire and a mushroom cloud rise from the place where Haman was standing. "Confirmed kill!"

Unfortunately, as is the case with the modern military tactic of drones striking terrorist compounds, there was collateral damage. Haman's entire household was put to death—Esther and Mordecai personally arranged for the executions. Never again would they or the rest of the Jews have to look over their shoulders out of fear of Haman's household.

* * *

Centuries after Haman's lifeless body hung on his own gallows, the apostle Peter referred to another Haman-like individual when he said, *"Honor the king"* (1 Peter 2:17). Peter was talking about Nero, emperor of Rome. A bad king. A ruthless, vicious, and unstable man. A murderous hater of Christians. Historical records tell us that Nero would light Christians on fire in his garden and would then have dinner with his guests while the martyrs burned on the lamp stands where they had been fastened. Yet Peter said to honor him. Why did he say that? Peter understood honor's function. It dismantles darkness. As long as there is honor in the land, the land has a chance to be redeemed. I believe Peter was being redemptive in asking the body of Christ to honor their chief persecutor. If believers prayed to get their hearts to a place where they could honor their adversary—something we can be certain Esther had to do as well—then they make room for God to enter the equation.

Honor brings Heaven into every situation in which we choose to act honorably. And when Heaven comes, people either become convicted or their hearts are hardened. First, love and mercy look for an opportunity to make an entrance even into the darkest of souls. If a person persists in wickedness, Heaven will act accordingly. Our job is to honor. Heaven's job is to sort things out so that justice and righteousness will prevail. Sometimes the only way for God to achieve that result is through direct missile strikes of weaponized honor Nero, like Haman, did not repent. He, too, was taken out.

* * *

Have I done it—painted targets through the leveraging of honor? Absolutely. Many times Before I had revelation on the subject, I painted targets unknowingly; now I do so strategically. Again—and I cannot emphasize this enough—this is never done with an intent to take people out. Our desire must always be reconciliation and restoration.

To say that the course we have chosen as a community of believers has met opposition is an understatement. I have personally faced accusation and reproach. At one point in our journey, a ministry in our area was strongly opposed to any move of God. They accused us of wrongdoing we had never committed and spread venomous rumors about our ministry. One rumor was that we fabricated signs and wonders—for example, that we would put glue on feathers and stick them on people's heads so they would look spiritual. Since when have feathers been gauges of spirituality? And glue?! Who conjures up such nonsense?

But that's what they said. After I'd had enough, I called a board meeting. I presented a formal resolution calling for our church to send financial gifts to the ministry that had attacked us. At the time, we didn't know anything about honor's ability to weaponize. We simply wanted to nurture a heart of forgiveness and grace. We asked for a meeting with the opposing ministry to resolve the matter. The result? Denied. So, we agreed to bless their ministry. At first my board could not understand my resolution. They questioned me. I quoted Jesus from his Sermon on the Mount: *"Love your enemies, bless those who curse you, do good to those who hate you, and pray for those who spitefully use you and persecute you, that you may be sons of your Father in heaven…"* (Matthew 5:44-45). "I want to be like my Father," I said to my colleagues, "and my Father instructed that, *'If your enemy is hungry, give him bread to eat; And if he is thirsty, give him water to drink; For so you will heap coals of fire on his head, And the Lord will reward you'*" (Proverbs 25:21-22).

I give to my enemies because if you love your enemies you will heap coals on their heads and make a way, through honor, for Heaven's intervention. When we started to send monthly support to that particular ministry, we received an email in which they asked, "Why did you send this to us? We do not need it or want it!" Surprisingly, they still cashed the checks—not just once, but for two years. After that time, that ministry fell apart. It ceased to exist in our area and its founders moved away to another state. That ministry had no business being there after it raised its voice against us. It was operating on the wrong platform; it had been built on the wrong foundation. We genuinely honored them, in spite of them, which allowed honor to weaponize and take them out. It was that simple. Honor works, as long as our motives are pure.

CHAPTER 6

REDEMPTION THROUGH HONOR

"For the weapons of our warfare are not carnal but mighty in God for pulling down strongholds" (2 Corinthians 10:4).
Honor is a powerful weapon in our spiritual arsenal, not for destruction, but for redemption.

* * *

I have had numerous encounters in the spirit realm. Most involve specific beings from heavenly realms. Not long ago I had unique encounter, not with a specific person, but with the burden an individual had carried in his heart almost two and a half thousand years ago. It was the burden of a king who paced the floor, who would not eat, who lay awake and would not allow any entertainment to come into his courts. The more I experienced that burden, the more I started to realize who that king was. The Scriptures confirmed my hunch. Let's look at the events of this historical account from the Book of Daniel, chapter 6. (Note: the *italicized text* below indicates direct quotations from the New King James Version; the full citation follows the story.)

***

The king was Darius, ruler over the Medeo-Persian Empire. Some of the king's counselors hated Daniel and plotted against him. They manipulated the king into signing a new law whereby the king's subjects could not pray to anyone except the king. Since Daniel prayed to God three times daily, it would be easy to catch him violating the law. When Daniel did indeed continue to pray in the manner he always had, the counselors seized the moment: *"And they went before the king, and spoke concerning the king's decree: 'Have you not signed a decree that every man who petitions any god or man within thirty days, except you, O king, shall be cast into the den of lions?'"*

The king, who had not discerned the motive behind the question, replied, *"The thing is true, according to the law of the Medes and Persians, which does not alter."*

Daniel's enemies found sufficient cause in that response to move in for the kill.

"So they answered and said before the king, 'That Daniel, who is one of the captives from Judah, does not show due regard for you, O king, or for the decree that you have signed, but makes his petition three times a day.'"

It was at that moment that the king began to carry the heavy burden for Daniel. *"And the king, when he heard these words, was greatly displeased with himself, and set his heart on Daniel to deliver him; and he labored till the going down of the sun to deliver him.*

"Then these men approached the king, and said to the king, 'Know, O king, that it is the law of the Medes and Persians that no decree or statute which the king establishes may be changed.'"

The king was distraught, but there was nothing he could do—the law demanded that Daniel be put to death.

"So the king gave the command, and they brought Daniel and cast him into the den of lions. But the king spoke, saying to Daniel, 'Your God, whom you serve continually, He will deliver you.' Then a stone was brought and laid on the mouth of the den, and the king sealed it with

his own signet ring and with the signets of his lords, that the purpose concerning Daniel might not be changed.

"Now the king went to his palace and spent the night fasting; and no musicians were brought before him. Also his sleep went from him."

(*From Daniel 6:12-18*; added commentary, mine).

* * *

For reasons I do not know, I felt Darius's burden for several nights in a row. I thought the burden was for Daniel, but it was revealed to me that the king was mostly burdened for himself and for his empire. Darius could not eat, sleep, or enjoy the pleasures of life while Daniel was in that den, because the king could not imagine life without his best counselor, and he felt his kingdom could not survive without Daniel. Can you imagine having relationship with kings of this world—not just rulers who hold a scepter, but all who govern realms of influence—to the extent where they pace the floors at night, concerned with our wellbeing, because they feel they cannot do what they do without us? Can you imagine a place where we are friends of kings to the point we are indispensable to them and to their kingdoms?

Every king around Darius had told him that he had an ally in Daniel. Darius had a friend and trusted confidant in Daniel. He had a mentor, a counselor, a priest and a prophet in Daniel. He needed him. Remember the king before Darius, Belshazzar, who had a party where all were drinking wine and having a great time? He decided to bring the vessels that came from the house of the Lord that Nebuchadnezzar had taken when they sacked Jerusalem and destroyed the temple. King Belshazzar took the party to a whole new level by drinking out of the golden temple vessels—holy unto the Lord. This was a mistake of monumental proportions! *"In the same hour the fingers of a man's hand appeared and wrote opposite the lampstand on the plaster of the wall of the king's palace; and the king saw the part of the hand that wrote"* (Daniel 5:5).

Belshazzar was a man who had already met Daniel. He had a vision and Daniel had interpreted it for him and said to him, *"My lord, may the dream concern those who hate you, and its interpretation concern your enemies!"* (Daniel 4:19). Daniel had interpreted the dream with such grace and redemptive power that the king knew he was safe with Daniel. While he was having his great party, the king's countenance changed and his thoughts troubled him. So that the joints of his hips loosened and his knees knocked against each other.

> *The king cried aloud to bring in the astrologers, the Chaldeans, and the soothsayers. The king spoke, saying to the wise men of Babylon, "Whoever reads this writing, and tells me its interpretation, shall be clothed with purple and have a chain of gold around his neck; and he shall be the third ruler in the kingdom." Now all the king's wise men came, but they could not read the writing, or make known to the king its interpretation. Then King Belshazzar was greatly troubled, his countenance was changed, and his lords were astonished.*

> *The queen, because of the words of the king and his lords, came to the banquet hall. The queen spoke, saying, "O king, live forever! Do not let your thoughts trouble you, nor let your countenance change. There is a man in your kingdom in whom is the Spirit of the Holy God. And in the days of your father, light and understanding and wisdom, like the wisdom of the gods, were found in him; and King Nebuchadnezzar your father—your father the king—made him chief of the magicians, astrologers, Chaldeans, and soothsayers. Inasmuch as an excellent spirit, knowledge, understanding, interpreting dreams, solving riddles, and explaining enigmas were found in this Daniel, whom the king named Belteshazzar, now let Daniel be called, and he will give the interpretation."* (Daniel 5:7-12).

They brought Daniel in before the king and Daniel read what was on the wall. He did not want to interpret it. They were drinking out of the vessels that came from the temple of the Lord. Daniel had been kidnapped from that land and made a eunuch in the courts of Nebuchadnezzar to serve those heathen kings. This could have been Daniel's moment of vengeance when he would rise up to pronounce judgment on that heathen kingdom which had imprisoned him, but Daniel did not even want to speak forth what was being revealed to him.

The king said, *"Whoever reads this writing, and tells me its interpretation, shall be clothed with purple and have a chain of gold around his neck; and he shall be the third ruler in the kingdom"* (Daniel 5:7).

The king knew that even if it was judgement, if it came out of the mouth of Daniel, there would still be hope. Can you imagine that kind of status and power in the world? Where the kings and rulers of realms of influence want us to speak, even if they know that our words could be an indictment from Heaven, and can put a demand on them to change. We might not really want to speak but what is on our hearts is from Heaven. *"He who loves purity of heart And has grace on his lips, The king will be his friend"* (Proverbs 22:11).

I have been blessed with many relationships with powerful and influential leaders. Most of those leaders have no need for material things. What they all need are trusted friends, men and women who will honor them by looking past their flaws and failures Kings desire relationship with the Daniels of their domain—the true friends of God and kings, whose perspective is always redemption, never condemnation.

Redeeming Kingdoms

We find additional strong scriptural emphasis for a redemptive mindset in one of the encounters John writes about in the book of Revelation. *"Then the seventh angel sounded: And there were loud voices in heaven, saying, 'The kingdoms of this world have become the kingdoms of our Lord and of His Christ, and He shall reign forever and ever!'"* (Revelation 11:15).

What John witnessed in Heaven at that moment was a completed process—a phenomenon that is way out there on the timeline, in the future. The kingdoms of this world had become the kingdoms of our Lord. And because of what John saw, he knew what his responsibility was to help facilitate that outcome, which would affect ours. We all have the responsibility as sons to bring forth the transfer of the kingdoms of this world to the jurisdiction of Jesus Christ. Like Daniel, we need to take a redemptive posture whereby we stand in the gap and we enable the kingdoms of this world to become the kingdoms of our Lord.

The kingdoms of this world described in Revelation are not nations, necessarily. Rather, they are realms of influence. In Silicon Valley area of California alone, there are numerous kingdoms: Apple, Google, Twitter, Facebook, IBM, and Yahoo. Hollywood is a kingdom. Amazon is a kingdom. Think of similar kingdoms across the nations. Several Swiss banks are kingdoms. Oil giants in the Middle East, German car manufacturers, and massive airlines are all kingdoms. You get the picture. Many of these realms of influence have a greater impact and are larger in financial substance than entire countries

John felt a responsibility resting on his shoulders. He was not called to be there as a passive observer. He was not shown all of these things just to tell us about what happens in Heaven, but to be a doorway enabling us to step into them. We are called to the responsibility of manifesting God's Kingdom in a way that provokes the kingdoms of this world to jealousy, stirring up a desire in them to turn towards Jesus. This outcome will not be produced by engaging with judgment, accusation and pointing fingers, or by pointing out wrong and preaching from soapboxes.

Honor will be the catalytic force for change in kingdoms of this world, because honor facilitates relationships. As we honor what is good in these kingdoms, we will have a greater opportunity to establish relationships which will be the vehicles for transformation.

I grew up in an excellent family. I never knew dysfunction until I began to follow Christ and went to church. Hypocrisy and the fear of man were the worst evils I encountered. Wherever this attitude prevails, honor is nowhere near.

A Suit and Tie Dilemma

I was recently invited to speak at a specific function. During the evening the people enjoyed my stories and were receiving what the Lord had put on my heart for them, until a certain man walked in. He was formally dressed in a suit and tie. In taking stock of the situation, he started making pointed comments to the host about my not wearing a tie. He was not an official leader of the community but he seemed to hold relational authority over the people. Everyone seemed concerned with what he thought about my story. The atmosphere instantly changed after he came in and I knew I had a decision to make. Either I would have to put up with his attitude all night, and that would make for a long night, or I had to deal with it immediately. I chose the latter.

I turned to the man with the love of God on my face and a genuine smile and said to him, "Brother, ties cannot preach! I have tried ties and I have tried suits but they just do not convey the message." The guy cracked a smile and extended his hand. That night he was set free from a religious spirit. While I was speaking, his hands were raised the whole time. He was tracking with me and the Lord set him free. What I said to him was not a spur of the moment thought—it came from a lifetime of being gracious to others like him. He could see I loved him and that I was not correcting him. He knew that I was not defending myself. We need to change some of our attitudes and things we are doing so that we appeal to and win over the kingdoms of this world.

The Experiment

The kingdoms of this world should be inspired by the honor and love we carry in our hearts. *"By this all will know that you are My disciples, if you have love for one another"* (John 13:35).

A couple of years ago I conducted a personal experiment to see if transmitting love really works. My goal was not to deny Christ but to avoid the subject. En route to the airport, I was picked up in a nondescript place so nobody would know who I was. The limo driver began to tell me his life story. I was surprised he spoke with me so openly, because limo drivers are instructed by their employers to be quiet and only speak if the client initiates conversation. For some reason, he began to tell me all about his life, his journey, and his troubles. I just listened.

After a while he asked me if I was a priest. I had not said a word all this time. When I told him I was not a priest, he said that I should be. Asking him why he had said that, he replied that there was something in me he could not explain that made him want to open up to me. Then he asked me about my life. So, I told him I do consulting work and write spy thrillers, purposefully avoiding the subject of faith. When we got to the airport, as I got out of the car, he asked me if I would pray for him. There had not been one moment's conversation about prayer. Not one thing that I said would have given him the impression that I have ever prayed. I just wanted to see if he would be touched by the presence of the Lord without my bringing up the subject. I wanted to be so full of love for this man that Christ in me would overflow and the hope of glory would fill his car with rivers of living water without my ever quoting even one verse of scripture or sounding like I was preaching.

It was an amazing testimony to me that as I got out he asked me to pray for him. When I agreed to pray on the flight, he urged me instead to pray with him straight away before I left! He was strategic. He decided we would both stand behind the car so it looked like we were unloading, because drivers are not allowed to sit at the airport pickup area for a long time. He asked me to act like we were unloading my stuff, but to place a hand on his shoulder and pray for him. The power of God started hitting him and I got scared. I was booked on a flight with people I could see arriving, and here was the limo driver shaking and swaying back and forth under the Holy Spirit's power!

I call it effortless evangelism. No probing questions, exhortations, or sermons. No awkwardness in the room because we just mentioned the name of Jesus. We simply live our lives for God to the fullest and we shine for Him in a way that draws people to Jesus through us.

Acquiring Kingdoms

On the flip side of this assignment to broker the transfer of the kingdoms of this world to Jesus, we have to enrich the kingdoms of our world with our in input and contributions. The kingdoms of this world became the kingdoms of our Lord because at some point these realms of influence became desirable to Him—"irresistible" as my friend Matthew Rudolph puts it. When we honor what is noteworthy and excellent in the world, we obtain access through relationship. Thus, we have opportunity to add value to the systems and rulers of this world.

Perhaps some of us who operate at a high level of business and manage acquisitions know that the acquisition of companies involves a faceted process that requires a lot of protocol. I have a friend experienced in company acquisitions. Many companies are willing to pay for the right to be the chief negotiating company for such an acquisition. That is where they begin and from there it goes into contract signing, due diligence for nine months to a year, and then they have to report back. They have lawyers and accountants go through the whole process with a fine-toothed comb.

Desire starts the whole process—the desire of one company to acquire another one. At the heart of our Savior, at the heart of the King of this Kingdom, Yeshua, is a desire for the kingdoms of this world to be a part of His kingdom. He does not see them for the wrong that they may be doing. He sees them for what they can become. That is how he saw you and me. He did not see us for what we were not doing. It is all about perspective. His perspective for you and me is redemptive. He sees the power that He has invested in us through His sacrifice, through His work, through His teachings, through the working of the Holy Spirit in our lives, and He sees what we can become.

I do not hear Jesus condemning this world—He never has! Like a forbearing, loving parent to a wayward child, the Lord says this: "I know that you are a mess right now, but this is just a temporary phase, because I see you coming into greatness. I see you with pure waters flowing through your whole being and I see all of Heaven coming around you to bolster you up."

The Role of a Redemptive Presence

It is because Daniel lived with a redemptive perspective that the king could not sleep that night. The kings of that land could not live without Daniel. They could not govern without him. He made the Kingdom of our Lord appealing to them.

And when he came to the den, he cried out with a lamenting voice to Daniel. The king spoke, saying to Daniel, "Daniel, servant of the living God, has your God, whom you serve continually, been able to deliver you from the lions?"

Then Daniel said to the king, "O king, live forever! My God sent His angel and shut the lions' mouths, so that they have not hurt me, because I was found innocent before Him; and also, O king, I have done no wrong before you."

Now the king was exceedingly glad for him, and commanded that they should take Daniel up out of the den. So Daniel was taken up out of the den, and no injury whatever was found on him, because he believed in his God (Daniel 6:20-23).

Have you ever wondered what Daniel's innocence was in God's eyes? Do you think it was about the sins that the religious church has always emphasized and over warned us to look out for—vices of greed, lust, and substance abuse? I believe the innocence found in Daniel was that he did not judge the heathen kings, thus affording them the opportunity to turn around. He was found innocent because he did not hold *these things* against them, even the men who threw him into the lion's den. He did not hold it against them, but continued to walk graciously before the Lord on their behalf. The only chance that they had was through Daniel, and today, the only chance they may have is through you and me.

Then King Darius wrote:

To all peoples, nations, and languages that dwell in all the earth: Peace be multiplied to you. I make a decree that in every dominion of my kingdom men must tremble and fear before the God of Daniel.

For He is the living God,
And steadfast forever;
His kingdom is the one which shall not be destroyed,
And His dominion shall endure to the end.
He delivers and rescues,
And He works signs and wonders
In heaven and on earth,
Who has delivered Daniel from the power of the lions.

So this Daniel prospered in the reign of Darius and in the reign of Cyrus the Persian (Daniel 6:25-28).

The king does not need a preacher to teach him what to say: the Spirit of the Living God is now activated in him to be able to know who he really is. He knows he is really there because there is a Daniel in the kingdom who has walked with kings like him in grace and purity of the Living God. The king recognizes that Daniel's God is steadfast forever, that His Kingdom is the one that shall not be destroyed, and His dominion shall endure to the end.

Protocol and Judgment

We do things differently these days and I am not suggesting we act as Darius did. We have the grace to walk in a redemptive way. As Jesus said, *"If you forgive the sins of any, they are forgiven..."* (John 20:23). That is the responsibility that we have been given. There is no place for us to pronounce judgment on cities or nations. If anybody has that assignment (and I believe that some do), the proclamations should be delivered with fear and trembling—not by some overly zealous preacher who gets up on Sunday and points his finger in the direction of California and says, "There is going to be an earthquake in California!" Doing so does not bring redemption, life, or transformative power. We cannot go along with that. We cannot speak judgment over our families. We cannot speak judgment over our children. We cannot speak judgment over our nation. If anything, we should pray, *"...In wrath, remember mercy"* (Habakkuk. 3:2).

We need to be the people whom the kings of this earth seek out because they know that no matter what, we are going to have honor in our actions, grace on our lips, and purity in our hearts.

It says in the Bible,

When you sit down to eat with a ruler,
Consider carefully what is before you;
And put a knife to your throat
If you are a man given to appetite.
Do not desire his delicacies,
For they are deceptive food (Proverbs 23:1-3).

I believe this deception has nothing to do with food and the deception does not come from the ruler. The deception comes from misunderstanding the setting we are in.

When the proverb exhorts us to think carefully about what is before us, it is not talking about food. Rather, it is exhorting us to consider carefully that there is a king before us. You can leave the palace and go somewhere later to eat, but at the palace, you have a king in front of you.

We have kings in front of us. They may not have scepters or be sitting on seats of power that look like thrones, but I promise they are all around us. They are kings of realms of influence and we must walk in such a way that we value the moments we get to share with them, be it in an elevator, be it on a car ride, be it in an Uber. You may not know them when you start the ride, but you are sitting next to them. We are called to the privilege of being friends of kings and this activates the kingly in us—the capacity on our lives that we are supposed to walk in. Jesus *"...has made us kings and priests to His God and Father, to Him be glory and dominion forever and ever"* (Revelation 1:6). There is a dimension of greatness that will manifest around us, as we facilitate leadership like kings.

We must not judge or accuse others to feel better about ourselves, but instead rightly divide the Word of Truth. As we know, the first thing that Solomon ever did was to give judgment about a baby:

Now two women who were harlots came to the king, and stood before him. And one woman said, "O my lord, ... this woman's son died in the night, because she lay on him. So she arose in the middle of the night and took my son from my side, while your maidservant slept, and laid him in her bosom, and laid her dead child in my bosom. And when I rose in the morning to nurse my son, there he was, dead. But when I had examined him in the morning, indeed, he was not my son whom I had borne."

And the king said, "The one says, 'This is my son, who lives, and your son is the dead one'; and the other says, 'No! But your son is the dead one, and my son is the living one.'" Then the king said, "Bring me a sword." So they brought a sword before the king. And the king said, "Divide the living child in two, and give half to one, and half to the other."

Then the woman whose son was living spoke to the king, for she yearned with compassion for her son; and she said, "O my lord, give her the living child, and by no means kill him!"

But the other said, "Let him be neither mine nor yours, but divide him."

So the king answered and said, "Give the first woman the living child, and by no means kill him; she is his mother."

And all Israel heard of the judgment which the king had rendered; and they feared the king, for they saw that the wisdom of God was in him to administer justice (1 Kings 3:16-17; 19-21; 23-28).

It was this wisdom that showed all of Israel he was called to succeed David. Can you imagine following David as king? For forty years, David, a man after God's own heart, was leading Israel. For forty years, he did all things well and the Bible says *"...he shepherded them according to the integrity of his heart, And guided them by the skillfulness of his hands"* (Psalms 78:72).

For forty years David destroyed every enemy all around them so that Solomon could succeed to the throne and inherit peace. David ordained an offering that was massive and given with joy, to build the temple, which created huge rejoicing in Israel (1 Chronicles 29:8-9). Can you imagine following David, whose first official act as king was to write a dirge and ask all of Israel to sing it to honor Saul, who threw spears at him from cave to cave and hunted him like a wild animal (2 Samuel 1:17-27). Solomon follows his father and does what David tells him to do.

We are living in days where there is a measure of government and kingly authority that is coming to the sons, not just to the Solomons with scepters and thrones, but to the sons of God, who know their places. We have been reborn into greatness, from eternal greatness, to turn anything that is not greatness into the greatness that we knew in eternity. The Seven Spirits of God are not teaching us what is here and how to work with what is here. They are reminding us of what we knew *there* from before, so we can bring *that* here. Then *this* on the earth begins to look like *that*, so *that* can land on *this* and there will be no separation of Heaven and earth—just as it was in the day Solomon dedicated the temple. *"And it came to pass, when the priests came out of the holy place, that the cloud filled the house of the Lord, so that the priests could not continue ministering because of the cloud; for the glory of the Lord filled the house of the Lord"* (1 Kings 8:10-11). The manifestation of Heaven in that place with the glory being infused into every facet of society during Solomon's day—that is possible for us today.

Isaiah said,

Arise, shine; For your light has come! And the glory of the Lord is risen upon you. For behold, the darkness shall cover the earth, And deep darkness the people; But the Lord will arise over you, And His glory will be seen upon you. The Gentiles shall come to your light, And kings to the brightness of your rising (Isaiah 60:1-3).

Isaiah was not prophesying something that had not happened before. He was talking about what he had already seen. It is possible for us to see it again. We have to walk in it by being redemptive, by truly loving this world, and by ridding ourselves of spiritual bigotry that has been in the church for so long. We cannot think that only we have the answers and the solutions, or that we are the only ones who are pure. I know people who have never set foot in a church, who have never had a part of anything that we are doing, but who walk in an exemplary and inspiring honor and righteousness. There is good out there for us to tap into and to elevate to a greater place. That is how we will be rid of evil in the world—not by saying it is so bad, but by saying and showing that it can be so much better.

Chapter 7

The Anatomy of Apology

As agents of redemption and transformation we must continually grow in our ability to ask for and release forgiveness.

Recently, I went to Singapore where Ian Clayton and I held a conference for Watchman Ngiam. We hold similar conferences together in various corners of the world. I am most grateful for the opportunity to travel and minister across the globe, especially when I can work alongside individuals of great stature and character such as Ian.

Regardless of the assignment, when I minister in different conferences and settings, I am well put-together. I am prayed up, I have prepared my heart, and I do my best to walk in a high level of excellence in my dealings with everyone involved. Conference attendees see the best of me. The matters I may grapple with at home, or areas of life in which I may face challenges, are generally not what I present when I am holding a microphone in front of a crowd. Though I try to maintain a level of personal transparency in my teaching, conferences are not the ideal setting to address some of my failings and the lessons I have learned from them. A book like this however, is more appropriate.

In this chapter I want to explore, even cathartically, the need we have to seek forgiveness due to bad decisions and wrong actions or attitudes. Furthermore, I would like us to consider a proper reconciliation process—one that begins with a sincere apology.

How to honorably apologize and seek forgiveness is one of the most significant things I have been learning while leading an ecclesiastical house in the United States for more than twelve years. At the same time, I have travelled around the earth interacting with leaders in multiple settings: corporate, government, military, law-enforcement, and the marketplace, among others. Making mistakes, hurting people around us, and being hurt by other's actions is inevitable. Therefore, we must know the proper way to deal with such matters. What I find shocking is that very few people know how to properly apologize and make amends.

My approach is that of a son who fails often. At the time of writing this manuscript, my wife and I are raising three teenagers. If I ever start to forget that I fail a lot, those three teenagers will be sure to remind me that I fail and make mistakes. It is from my children, my wife, and the people closest to me whom I have to ask for forgiveness the most. Rarely will I be in a conference and have the need to ask forgiveness from the crowd or hosts. It is at home, in my office, and with the people I most rub shoulders with—sometimes scraping and scratching inadvertently—or because of a mistake in judgment that I fail. In such moments of failure, I humble myself and ask for forgiveness.

Think of an apology as a song comprised of verse and chorus. Some songs begin with a chorus and then we hear the verse; sometimes the verse comes first and the chorus follows. If the anatomy of an apology is like the composition of a song, then the chorus is the part where we say we are sorry and the verse is the part where we commit ourselves to show the fruit of repentance. In either case, it is of utmost importance that our apology is simple and genuine. No excuses, explanations, or justifications, but a wholehearted and sincere confession: "I was wrong." Then we say something like this: "I am sorry. Will you please forgive me?" That's it. Nothing more needs to be said or done for the "chorus" of the apology.

The Admirable Prodigal

One of the most outstanding examples of repentance is found in the story of the prodigal son in Luke 15. I admire the prodigal son for several reasons. Unfortunately, the religious church has only presented this young man negatively, until he is restored to his father, that is. I understand that the prodigal son made a bad choice and pursued a course of destruction. In that sense, we should not emulate the prodigal son. Who wants to waste their inheritance? Who wants to work in a pig pen, wishing he could eat what the pigs are eating? No one wants that life. But I think the prodigal has some remarkable qualities the religious church has overlooked. The first misconception lies with the primary purpose for which Jesus told the parable—it was not to highlight the prodigal nature of the son, but rather the goodness of the father. Jesus told the story because religious people accused Him of sitting and eating with winos and sinners. He wanted to explain his motive for interacting with such people. He told the story to set the record straight.

We should recognize the admirable qualities in the prodigal son. First and foremost, the prodigal knew he had an inheritance and he put a demand on it. So many followers of Christ do not recognize or value their inheritance. They walk around like paupers, not sons. We are facing an orphan spirit and a poverty mindset in so many places worldwide. There is a lack of self-respect, an ignorance of our identity as heirs of God and joint heirs with Jesus, and a failure to properly engage with the responsibility of exercising dominion over creation. We walk around wishing we had a dad Who loved us; wishing we had a dad who gave us stuff; wishing we had more, instead of recognizing that we can be the change we want to see—that we can help facilitate the very realm we want to live in and govern.

The prodigal recognized his inheritance and he asked for it. Yes, he claimed it prematurely and then wasted it, but at least he acknowledged that it was available to him in the father. The prodigal's most admirable quality is seen after his failure, during the time he spent in the pig pen. The text reads, *"... He came to himself..."* (Luke 15:17). When we make mistakes, we need to reach a moment in which we come to ourselves, a moment when we have enough integrity and courage to admit that the way we are operating does not represent the goodness of God and Heaven's deposits in our lives. That is what happened with the prodigal. He was in the pig pen and he came to the place where I imagine he might have said to himself, "This is not me! I am living among the pigs while there is so much more available to me in my father's house—so much so, that even the lowest paid worker has more than enough."

The next part is even more critical, and thus more of an admirable quality in the prodigal: he made a decision to turn around and make things right. He made a choice to repent, to do an about face, to turn and go in the right direction again. That is what the prodigal did: he said, *"I will arise and go to my father, and will say to him, 'Father, I have sinned against heaven and before you, and I am no longer worthy to be called your son. Make me like one of your hired servants'"* (Luke 15:18-19). And in that statement lies the full composition, chorus and verse, of an apology. Again, the chorus in our illustration is, "I was wrong. Please forgive me," and the verse, "I will make this right now. I will show the fruit of repentance." No explanations, no excuses, no blame-shifts. Simply and sincerely we admit wrongdoing and commit to a process of reconciliation.

John the Baptist said to the Pharisees, the tax collectors, the soldiers and to the people who gathered around him, *"Brood of vipers! Who warned you to flee from the wrath to come? …And even now the ax is laid to the root of the trees"* (Luke 3:7, 9). It is interesting that he specified the ax is laid at the *root* of the trees. He did not say at the *base* of the tree. The reason the ax is laid at the root of the tree is because the roots are beneath the surface. The source of wrongdoing is beneath the surface: it is the stuff that nobody sees. We have to be real with ourselves and say, "There is some stuff that nobody sees that is wrong in me that is causing me to make these mistakes and have these attitudes that I need to repent of, so I need to come clean. I need the ax at the root of this tree."

John the Baptist advised, *"…Bear fruits worthy of repentance…"* (Luke 3:8). Mature sons manifest fruit worthy of repentance. The prodigal son says, "I am returning home and I want to be one of your lowest paid workers. I am willing to start at the very bottom. I want to show you Dad, that I am truly sorry. I do not just want to say it; I want to prove it. Give me a chance to come back as one of the lowest paid workers."

Forgiveness and the Restoration of Relationships

I come across many cases in which people struggle with making a simple heartfelt apology for their wrongdoing. Generally, an apology goes like this: "I am so sorry you feel this way." That is not an apology, for it basically says, "I am so sorry that your own issues and misperceptions cause you to think I am wrong." An apology is when we recognize our wrongdoing or our mistake and we say, "I hurt you. I was wrong. I own this. Please forgive me." Then stop talking. If they have the heart to forgive us, they do so, and we move on. Then as we bear fruit of repentance the relationship has a chance to be restored. We must understand that our repentance does not guarantee an immediate return to the state of relationship before the offense. Often, a time of reconciliation is needed.

Honor must be present in the conflict resolution process in another way: the matter must remain private between those needing to resolve it. It must not spread to others. One of the core values that help govern interactions at our church is that of resolving conflict according to the way Jesus taught. *"If your brother sins against you, go and tell him his fault between you and him alone. If he hears you, you have gained your brother"* (Matthew 18:15). You go to the brother. You do not go to another leader or another person and you do not start pulling others into the mix, thus spreading seeds of discord. You go directly to the person and simply state the matter: "I feel sinned against in this area, you said this, you did this, your attitude was this and it hurt me, it insulted me. I feel sinned against. Will you consider making this right?" Sometimes the other person does not feel the same way and says, "Well I do not think I did anything wrong." So we say, "OK, let's pray and come back in a week and talk about this again." If that does not work we say, "OK, let's fast for some time and come back and discuss this again." Trust me, usually it gets resolved before we need to fast!

We have learned that if we commit ourselves to this very simple process of bringing wrongdoing before the person who wronged us and having a heart that is open to forgive, issues are resolved quickly. It is rare that I as a senior leader of our church get involved with matters between our staff or between individuals in the church. Even so, by the time a matter comes to me, there is much heavenly input surrounding the issue due to the proper steps taken up until that point. We, as a culture, have learned to honor and value each other. Part of honoring has to do with being able to recognize wrongdoing, to ask for forgiveness, to give forgiveness, to release people, to let it go and not bring it back up again.

A Sincere Apology

I am going to end with this. A few months ago, I was finishing a novel, *The Cargo*, that I had been working on. I stopped travelling for a couple of months in order to finish the book. I focused much of my time on it, so I was gone a lot. I was leaving at three in the morning. I was coming home at midnight. Even though I was home, this was a season when I was not truly present at home.

When I completed the novel I realized that there was a distance between me and my kids and even my wife, even though I was staying in the same house with them and we were eating dinner around the table every night. But I was not truly present because my mind was so focused on getting the project done. There were things that crept in during that time that I found myself being wrong about in my attitude and my responses. I was short and sharp. I was not kind. I was not sweet-spirited towards my family. I was distant and I was not present for important things in their lives. A lot of issues flew under the radar when I should have been more attentive to them.

There came a moment when I realized there was only one way out. There was only one way to properly deal with the problem. I gathered my children in my room and I asked them to sit on the bed. Because my wife was not there at the time, I recorded the interaction so I could play it back for her. I remember looking each one of my children in the eyes and apologizing to each one of them for specific things that I had done wrong. Then I said to them overall as a group: "I was wrong the last few months in these areas and I ask you to forgive me. I am so sorry for this, this, this, and this." It was a very tough conversation because of some of the things that happened in the process of us bumping against each other were where I had felt wronged by them. But I owned the responsibility, as the adult, as a parent, and as a mature son, to deal with my stuff and to own my part of it. I did not make it about what they had done that hurt me, or bring that up to justify my wrong actions. Instead I took the responsibility to own the issue because I wanted it to be dwelt with. I remember apologizing, and then one after another, the kids not only forgave me but they owned their individual parts without me ever having to bring up their actions.

That is the amazing thing. When we align with the ways of the Kingdom everything comes into alignment. When we align with God's heart, things that we do not even touch get dealt with. I was able to resolve things with my children, but the best part of all of this was that I had recorded it. I played the recording back to my wife, Danielle, while we sat in the car. In twenty-one years of marriage I have never seen such admiration and respect in my wife's eyes towards me as I did that day. She looked at me with the expression, "You are my man."

It is a powerful place to be in when a husband and wife repent in front of their children and each other, friends repent in front of each other, or leaders repent in front of people they are leading. It is a position from which we can exercise dominion on the earth. True government, the government of God, is established on honor, righteousness, justice, mercy, and truth. The anatomy of an apology has all those qualities woven into it.

So, if there is someone you need to forgive or someone you need to confront because you feel wronged, do it today. But remember, it is best left simple, it does not need to be lengthy, it should not be convoluted or multifaceted. "I feel sinned against," or "Please forgive me." It is simply that. If it comes from an honorable, pure heart, backed with prayer, backed with the engaging of Heaven in the process, it will have results and it will bear fruit. You will then be able to bear fruit worthy of repentance and worthy of forgiveness. And we will all advance from strength to strength, from faith to faith, from victory to victory, and from glory to glory.

CHAPTER 8

DIRGES FOR SPEAR-THROWERS

The Bible records more than twenty attempts on David's life by King Saul. David lived as a fugitive for years, hiding from cave to cave. On several occasions, David's life was in such grave danger that he even sought refuge among Israel's enemies, the Philistines. But one day, all the running came to an end. A man bearing news of Saul's demise came to David. The king was dead and so was his son Jonathan. David was no longer an outlaw, but a king about to embark on a forty-year reign in Israel. Saul was gone. David was free. But David's response to the news was unexpected, to say the least.

David did not rejoice over King Saul's demise. He did not express relief that his archenemy was dead, nor did he celebrate the fact he would now become king. Rather,

Then David lamented with this lamentation over Saul and over Jonathan his son, and he told them to teach the children of Judah the Song of the Bow...

"The beauty of Israel is slain on your high places!
How the mighty have fallen!

WEAPONIZED HONOR

Tell it not in Gath,
Proclaim it not in the streets of Ashkelon—
Lest the daughters of the Philistines rejoice,
Lest the daughters of the uncircumcised triumph.

"O mountains of Gilboa,
Let there be no dew nor rain upon you,
Nor fields of offerings.
For the shield of the mighty is cast away there!
The shield of Saul, not anointed with oil.
From the blood of the slain,
From the fat of the mighty,
The bow of Jonathan did not turn back,
And the sword of Saul did not return empty.

"Saul and Jonathan were beloved and pleasant in their lives,
And in their death they were not divided;
They were swifter than eagles,
They were stronger than lions.

"O daughters of Israel, weep over Saul,
Who clothed you in scarlet, with luxury;
Who put ornaments of gold on your apparel.

"How the mighty have fallen in the midst of the battle!
Jonathan was slain in your high places
I am distressed for you, my brother Jonathan;
You have been very pleasant to me;
Your love to me was wonderful,
Surpassing the love of women

"How the mighty have fallen,
And the weapons of war perished!" (2 Samuel 1:17-27).

The song honors Saul. I find it amazing that David, a man viciously persecuted by the now-deceased king, would speak well of Saul and grieve over his loss. That David would refer to Saul (along with Jonathan) as *mighty, the beauty of Israel, beloved, swifter than eagles,* and *stronger than lions*—that David would exhort the daughters of Israel to mourn for the king *who clothed [them] in scarlet with luxury,* and *put ornaments of gold on [their] apparel*—I find it astonishing. Anyone who can sing a dirge over the person who threw spears at them is someone who operates at the highest level of honor and that person is qualified to rule.

The song itself is remarkable. However, there is another element we must consider. David did not compose the Song of the Bow after he learned of Saul's death. The fact he *"told them to teach…the Song of the Bow"* indicates that David had written the song beforehand. This means David wrote a song of honor for Saul while running for his life—at the very same time Saul was organizing and leading killing squads to eliminate him. In other words, David made a choice to honor Saul at the height of Saul's dishonorable behavior towards David.

There must have been times when the dirge David prepared to honor Saul's legacy gave David the reason to keep going. David had an appointment with honor and thus honor became a vehicle to take him safely down the timeline to that appointment. I can imagine David's men suggesting decisive action against the king who was out to destroy them. On two occasions recorded in the Scriptures we know the tables were turned on Saul—the hunter could have easily become the prey. But David refused to raise his hand against the king God had anointed. David knew that even though God regretted making Saul king, God had not yet removed him. Saul was king and David would honor him to the very end—and then some.

Part of the reason for David's restraint was his honor for Saul's position. But weaponized honor had a big part to play as well. David had a song to sing to honor the man who had dishonored him the most. Not only would David sing the song, he would teach it to the people. "No, brothers," I imagine David saying to his mighty men who were bent on vengeance. "We can't take this matter into our own hands. I have been working on this song…and I have to get to that moment when I sing it, when we all sing it, to honor Saul." We can find great encouragement and courage by envisioning future moments during which we plan to give honor. David carried the dirge for Saul in his heart and it gave him yet one more reason to stay alive.

Honor Where Honor is Due

The principle is equally powerful when we cultivate honor for those who truly deserve it. I was once invited to be one of the speakers at the graduation ceremony of a very prestigious school. The mayor of the town would be the keynote speaker. Other notable speakers and guests would be seated on either side of me in the front. The three months prior to the event were very difficult times for me. I was traveling constantly and I was facing various trials . There was at least one moment I can remember when I almost lost heart, but one fact kept me going. One more piece of information had been given to me on the day I was invited to speak: my parents would be attending. There is no one other than my wife Danielle to whom I am more indebted and grateful for than my mom and dad. I did not yet know what I would speak about, but I was certain of one thing: I would leverage my platform of influence on graduation night to honor my parents. I played out the scenario in my mind continually and during difficult flights or assignments, I found courage to persevere. Honor had been engaged and Honor was carrying me.

The pages of this book would never be enough to contain descriptions of the numerable honor scenarios I am cultivating in my heart at this very moment for my loved ones, but also for my enemies Yes, I have enemies, as David did—people who have maligned my name and who have raised their voice and hand against me unjustifiably. I have given myself over to God and to the tutelage of His servant, Honor. The Lord is coaching me through Honor. He is helping me win the battle from within and to imagine the very best results for the situations involving my enemies.

I have seen with my mind's eye moments when I meet up with those who have opposed me and we embrace, sincerely and wholeheartedly. I envision settings in which God's grace is applied to the matters that have brought dissension. I am not interested in winning an argument or being proven right in long-standing contentions. I only want reconciliation. Honor can do that. I have seen it many times. I am continually instructed in Heaven and by God's word to hold honor in my heart for my enemies. I stand before the Father often, holding them up in high regard by focusing on their good qualities. I have already experienced exceptional breakthrough in this area.

Reconciliation of Differences

One of the most notable reconciliations took place a few years ago. While I was on a missionary assignment halfway across the world, Danielle messaged me that something remarkable had just taken place. A couple that had left our church badly years earlier had sought reconciliation. The circumstances behind their change of heart were nothing short of miraculous. The couple had felt guilt for a long time for leaving us the way they did. There is a proper way to leave a church—with honor and respect going both ways between those departing and the church leadership and congregation. When people's time with us has, from Heaven's perspective, legitimately come to an end, there should be proper communication with leadership. Honor and gratitude should be moving in both directions—from them to us and vice versa. Then there should be a time of blessing and sending off, both privately and publicly.

In this case, the couple and their family had left very haphazardly, out of offense and suspicion. Conviction had set in and both the husband and wife regretted their actions. But they also felt things had gone too far to turn around. However, while I was on that overseas mission, two unusual things took place in the life of the couple's oldest daughter. First, she had a dream in which she saw her family and our family coming together. Second, she happened to be playing a phone game called Words with Friends. Her parents had only permitted her to play that game with close friends of hers from school or their new church, but for some unknown reason the settings on her phone shifted to a mode which allowed her to play with anyone in the world. When she clicked on the game, she would face an opponent who was on at the very same time in Russia, Egypt, or New Zealand. By amazing *God*-incidence her first opponent was our oldest son, Christos, with whom she had been friends while at our church, and who was definitely not on her list of approved friends for the game.

The girl ran into her parents' room and woke them up. She explained what had happened. They were deeply moved. The next day, they called Danielle, who then contacted me. Upon my return, we all met for sushi. After long embraces and many tears, we broke bread (well, raw fish) together and made things right.

From my perspective, the catalyst for the reconciliation was honor. When we reconnected, we discovered that even though things had gone badly years earlier, each couple had held the other couple in their hearts with honor: therefore,

Honor had a chance to do this work. It was one of the most glorious moments in my entire time of ministry. And it can happen again. I believe there will be many more great stories like mine and some of them will be your stories Honor is more powerful than dishonor. Love is stronger than hatred. I choose honor. I choose love and I invite you to join me.

* * *

People are not interested in following bitter, vengeful leaders. They prefer to follow individuals who are forgiving and gracious. Why? Because everyone knows that at some point, each of us fails. When a man like David chooses to honor and forgive Saul, the whole nation has hope that grace and mercy will be predominant forces, rather than judgment and retribution.

I end this chapter with a notable excerpt from US history. Arguably one of the most controversial decisions an American president has ever made was President Harry S. Truman's firing of General Douglas MacArthur in 1951. General MacArthur was a highly decorated war hero who played a significant role in the Pacific theater during World War II, particularly in the Philippines. He was a Medal of Honor recipient and one of only five men to become General in the US Army. Moreover, General MacArthur was assigned the command of United Nations forces fighting in the Korean War.

On April 11, 1951, President Truman relieved General MacArthur of his command, citing as cause the general's insubordination to the Commander in Chief (the President) and disparaging comments MacArthur had made about the President and his administration. As would be expected, Truman's decision precipitated a media frenzy and a massive outcry from millions of Americans. Though I have studied the historical facts surrounding this event extensively, I will not state my position in the matter at this time. My focus is the aftermath of MacArthur's firing.

Relieved from his command by the President, General MacArthur returned to the United States about two weeks later. He was received by a throng of people, half-a-million strong, in San Francisco. Within a few days, MacArthur flew to New York City where he was honored by the largest yet ticker-tape parade in US history. He continued from there to other large cities where he addressed large crowds. In each of the events that were held in his honor, General MacArthur spoke negatively of President Truman and his cabinet. The President, on the other hand, remained silent.

Even when strongly urged by his closest confidants to make a statement for the media, in which he would respond to MacArthur's accusations and allay the concerns of the wider US constituency, President Truman refused to speak one word to the media on the matter. When Secretary of State Dean Acheson pressed the President for a reason for his refusal to defend the firing of MacArthur, the President said he did not need to do anything about the matter, because MacArthur was doing the work for him. What Truman meant was that the general, through his toxic remarks directed towards the White House, was digging his own grave socially and politically. The President explained that people who were turning up to honor MacArthur would only sympathize with him and take his side for a short while. MacArthur's vicious lashing out against his superiors would eventually be deemed dishonorable and the crowds would dissipate. And that is exactly what happened. Within a few months, MacArthur could not even fill a movie theater. The American people were fed up with his attacks against their President.

Whether MacArthur was right or wrong in the matters pertaining to his release from military command is immaterial to us for the purposes of this book. However, the outcome of the general's tongue-lashings against the President at events and in the media illustrate the fact that people will not consistently follow disgruntled, bitter leaders. The President's silence demonstrated great wisdom and temperance, as well as insight in principles pertaining to honor.

Humanity gravitates towards honor because we were created by God, who is Love. When He made us, God deposited within us all expressions of His love, including honor. We are drawn to honor and we are inspired by it. Dishonor has the opposite effect. It turns us away. The Douglas-MacArthur incident proves this beautifully . Millions of people came out to honor the general for his outstanding service to his country. And, for a little while, they even lent an ear to hear him voice his complaints about the administration. Yet when it became clear that dishonor was taking over, the people scattered.

I share this historical fact to establish a proper setting to make this statement: in the eyes of the people of Israel, what qualified David as their leader more than anything else, was the Song of the Bow. Everyone knew David's story and what Saul had done to him. David's choice to carry a song of honor in his heart—one he would ask all of Israel to sing during a time of mourning for King Saul—demonstrated to Israel that David's transformation from shepherd to king was complete. He had a heart for God and through it, David was a man after God's own heart. They would go anywhere with him. They would celebrate and support David as their new king.

As a leader, very few things inspire, challenge, and motivate me more than the standard David set for honor. He raised the bar incredibly high. May you and I find the grace and integrity of heart to live according to that standard.

CHAPTER 9

HONOR'S REWARDS

Esther's story does not end with Haman and his sons hanging from Haman's own gallows or even with the Jews. *"On the day that the enemies of the Jews had hoped to overpower them, the opposite occurred, in that the Jews themselves overpowered those who hated them"* (Esther 9:1). In a way, this is only the beginning. Honor had weaponized: in cooperation with a brave queen and her wise kinsman, Honor eliminated Esther and Mordecai's archenemy. There was a second phase to Honor's operation: to lift Esther and Mordecai to positions of honor and prominence so they could exercise dominion over the entire kingdom. The biblical account of Queen Esther's story ends with references to Mordecai being *"...great in the king's palace, and his fame spread throughout all the provinces..."* (Esther 9:4), and Esther with him writing decrees and exercising *"full authority"* (Esther 9:29) in kingdom matters, including the annual remembrance of the Jews deliverance through the observance of the celebration of Purim. Having examined Honor's significant role in Esther's breakthrough and the Jews' deliverance, we can observe that Esther and Mordecai rise to positions of prominence and power. It becomes clear that honor and dominion or authority (*exousia* in Greek) are closely connected.

I propose that Honor's entanglement with humanity is not only to right wrongs and mete out respect to those who deserve it, but also to establish God's sons in their proper places of authority in His Kingdom. In other words, YHVH has assigned Honor with the task of empowering us, His sons, to govern: to rule the earth fully aware of our inheritance in Him.

Remarkably, honor has the capacity to unlock the limitless potential for greatness in each of us. When we give honor to friends or foes alike, we help facilitate alignment with their God-given potential and destiny; moreover, we co-labor with Heaven in YHVH's work of mercy and grace to bring out the best in everyone, even His enemies—keep in mind that *"The Lord is … not willing that any should perish but that all should come to repentance"* (2 Peter 3:9). Honor's primary objective is redemption, not destruction. Remember, even Haman had an opportunity to turn around and recognize his wrongdoing. Honor had weaponized and gave Haman the chance to repent or die. Haman held onto hatred and genocide, thus choosing death.

Releasing Greatness

In all the years I have engaged with Honor, the Holy Spirit has been teaching me how to leverage honor to bring out the best in people. One of the most inspiring aspects of Jesus's leadership over His disciples as their rabbi was his ability to demonstrate their greatness to them. He chose *"uneducated and untrained men"* (Acts 4:13) and commits Himself to make them fishers of men (Matthew 4:19). Jesus assigns important tasks to His disciples and he places trust and responsibility in them, in spite of the disciples' repeated mistakes and ignorance about Kingdom values For example, in Luke 9 the disciples demonstrate the wrong perspective numerous times: they desire to call fire down on cities that do not receive them, they forbid someone casting out demons in Jesus's name because the disciple argued, *"...he does not follow with us"* (Luke 9:49). Jesus patiently corrects the disciples and continues to give them responsibility. The first part of Luke 10 reads, *"After these things the Lord appointed seventy others also, and sent them two by two before His face into every city and place where He Himself was about to go"* (Luke 10:1).

The greatest honor Jesus gave His disciples was to entrust them with the establishment of His Church and the continuation of His work in the world. After His resurrection and immediately before His ascension, Jesus commissions His (now) apostles to disciple nations. He promises His power and protection over them and He empowers them by the Holy Spirit to be His *"witnesses in Jerusalem, and in all Judea, in Samaria, and to the end of the earth"* (Acts 1:8). Through a three-year equipping process, Jesus honors His disciples out of their mediocrity and limitations into fruitful ministry and world-changing impact. He brings out the best in them.

This facet of honor can also be seen in an incident in the life of the prophet Elisha. In 2 Kings 8, Ben-Hadad king of Syria was sick. When the king heard that Elisha had arrived in Damascus, he called his servant, Hazael, and said to him, *"Take a present in your hand, and go to meet the man of God, and inquire of the Lord by him, saying, 'Shall I recover from this disease?'"* (2 Kings 8:8). Hazael obeyed the king's wishes. He set out to meet with Elisha, and he brought a gift—well, not just one gift. The account indicates that the king's servant *"...took a present with him, of every good thing of Damascus, forty camel-loads..."* (2 Kings 8:9).

This servant's preparation for his encounter with Elisha is fascinating. The king told him to bring Elisha a present in his hand, then Hazael loaded forty camels with the finest products the city had to offer. Why? It was not because Elisha asked for these goods or needed them. Having forty camels' worth of anything is a logistical nightmare for an itinerant minister. I usually travel with two large suitcases and a carry-on. In European nations where many people own compact vehicles, transporting even my three pieces of luggage can be a stretch for my hosts. Can you imagine Elisha waking up to forty gift-bearing camels lined up outside his lodge? Hazael's gift to Elisha from the king is today's equivalent of forty car trunks full of presents. This gesture was not to meet a need or the prophet's demands. In fact, in another incident involving a Syrian general who was cured of leprosy, Elisha was emphatic about not receiving anything at all.

Ben-Hadad and Hazael brought the presents because they honored Elisha. They wanted him to know they esteemed him as a man of God, and they valued his time and gifting. A similar dynamic is seen during the height of Solomon's kingdom. The Bible says *"...all the earth sought the presence of Solomon to hear his wisdom, which God had put in his heart. Each man brought his present: articles of silver and gold, garments, armor, spices, horses, and mules, at a set rate year by year"* (1 Kings 10:24). Not only once—but consistently—kings brought gifts to Solomon. It surely was not because Solomon needed anything. There was enough gold and silver in Solomon's day to pave the roads with it. The kings brought the gifts to honor Solomon, just as Ben-Hadad and Hazael did for Elisha many years later.

We know that Hazael was inquiring about a life-or-death matter, but we also need to understand the way a prophet's gift operates. There is not only foretelling involved in prophesy, but also forth-telling. In other words, Elisha was not merely telling the future, he was co-laboring with Heaven to create it. No prophet operates beyond God's will and sovereignty, but prophets do have an important part in the execution and outcome of God's purposes. These presents were to show the prophet that he was valued, so that Elisha would operate at full capacity in his office and gifting. In Solomon's case, as the incident with the Queen of Sheba illustrates, kings sought audience with Solomon to ask him hard questions about the matters of their kingdoms and hearts. They wanted the King of Israel to take them seriously and to be at his very best.

When we host speakers at our church, we follow a protocol of presenting them with gift baskets and other small gifts upon their arrival. We eat at excellent restaurants and we communicate upfront matters pertaining to their compensation. In the case of foreign guests, we provide an iPhone and pocket money in US currency, so they can stay in touch with their families and not have to scramble to try to exchange money at a bank. In short, we take financial concerns out of the equation. We tell the speakers, "We will bless you. You will not have to trust God for provision from other sources for the work you are doing here among us—we will take good care of you." Immediately, our guests light up when they realize the preparation that has gone into honoring them. And come first meeting, they are edified, emotionally and spiritually. Following a thoughtful and heart-felt introduction from one of our pastors, they step into their speaking assignment, firing on all cylinders to release the fullness of what God has for all of us. It works every time—honor brings out the best in everyone and for everyone.

Our Enemies
One of the rewards of engaging with Honor and walking honorably even towards our enemies is that they get dealt with. Among the great promises of blessing that Moses declared to Israel is Deuteronomy 28:7: *"The Lord will cause your enemies who rise against you to be defeated before your face; they shall come out against you one way and flee before you seven ways."* It is my conviction, and I trust through the pages of this

book can be yours as well, that Honor has a part to play in the routing of our enemies. It was certainly so for Esther, Daniel, David and many other biblical heroes of our faith. When our enemies are thwarted the attitude of our heart is very important. Remember, our objective in "deploying" honor is never to see the destruction of our enemies, but to be catalytic through mercy, forgiveness and unconditional love to see restoration and peace—the Shalom of YHVH. The Bible holds keys for us in this area:

Do not rejoice when your enemy falls,
And do not let your heart be glad when he stumbles;
Lest the Lord see it, and it displease Him,
And He turn away His wrath from him (Proverbs 24:17-18).

Honor, working in conjunction with angelic forces and perhaps numerous other heavenly agents will obtain the victory for us over our enemies—those who oppose and resist us in our assignments for God. Our stance must be one of humility throughout the entire process. The Scriptures are clear here, that anything else would disrupt the plan God has to vindicate us and mete out justice.

Unfortunately, everything I am currently walking in as an individual, and also all that I participate in with family and the sons of God in the nations has come at a price. We have faced much opposition. We have had enemies. We still do. I am always more keen to have the right mind-set during seasons of accusations and attacks than I am to win. I have seen my enemies smashed to the ground many times. I choose not to share any examples, because I want to cover those involved. In each case, fear, the fear of the Lord grips my heart, not elation or satisfaction. I do not rehash in my mind all their wrongs towards me and my family and how they deserved what happened to them. Instead, I recognize that what happened to them can happen to me, unless I maintain an attitude of honor and respect, regardless of people's wrongs towards me.

I strongly urge you, my friend, to consider this stance. If you struggle to walk this way, as I admittedly have done so at times, I recommend this practical approach, comprised of the following:

1) Knowing, based on the verse above, that rejoicing over our enemy's fall will displease the Lord, it becomes clear that the opposite approach will please Him. We set our hearts to do what pleases our Father, and we evaluate our hearts against that standard.
2) We ask Holy Spirit to help us. We admit we have difficulty not saying, "Serves you right!" to our enemies, and we plead with heaven for forgiveness and for help. Holy Spirit has always answered that prayer for me. He will do it for you as well. The victory for us is so much greater than relief from the presenting circumstances. As we receive the heavenly perspective to see the person as held captive to the demonic influence that is using them to come at us (Ephesians 6:12), our victory also becomes theirs. We are empowered with the keys to vanquish the real enemy in the situation with heavenly weapons of compassion, honor, and all the components of love, against which the accuser has no law to use against us (Galatians 5:23). Not only is that battle won, but once we own the keys to that assault, it cannot ever be used against us again.

Overcoming evil is more a matter of our hearts being rightly aligned with God than it is applying book knowledge or clever tactics. If we keep our hearts pure, we will rise from within and bring victory into every situation.

Compound Returns

"Whoever cares for the poor makes a loan to the Eternal; such kindness will be repaid in full and with interest" (Proverbs 19:17 VOICE).

I used to be able to keep track of what I call "honor paybacks"—the heavenly-generated, multiplied returns on any investment we make into people through honor. I am unable to keep up any longer with such testimonies, not only from my own life, but also from others who walk closely with us and have caught on to this vision and are pursuing Honor diligently. The Bible clearly states that God honors those who honor Him and that what we give in His Name will be returned to us, with interest. It did not have to be that way, but that is how YHVH chooses to operate His economy. *"Give, and it will be given to you: good measure, pressed down, shaken together, and running over…"* (Luke 6:38).

I am richly blessed by an outstanding family, extended family, friends, church, and many other non-material blessings. I could go on forever about Honor's part in building the relationships that make me feel very wealthy in that regard. But I want to focus on material things as I close this book for a specific reason. Material things are important to me, not because I need *things* to feel valued or important, and not because of what material wealth can buy me. It is because material blessings are evident to the world around us as a quantifiable measure of success. For me, having an abundance of nice things is not necessary—I do not pursue abundance for the sake of having things. I pursue the fullness of all God has for me materially because wealth automatically gives us influence in places where our influence counts the most—among the influential.

I always remember this example: When we bought our first

high-end European car, I took a friend for a ride. I let him drive the car. He was a friend who loved us and valued us; however, I do not think I ever had much influence on him. About a month after he drove my car, I happened to be at a social gathering where this friend was surrounded by a group of people in casual conversation. From an adjoining room, I overheard my friend starting a sentence with, "Well, Marios says…" I could not believe it—I was being quoted. I promise you that this would not have happened before my new car purchase. My friend's perception of me had changed, and through him, so had the perception of everyone in the room.

Do I like the way we measure success and even ascribe value to people because of what they own? No, I do not, but that is the way things are in this world. No one of influence consistently seeks counsel from the poor. Being blessed by God with material things is a door-opener for us, and, in that regard, Honor is the doorkeeper.

In 1990, following my time in the Cypriot Special Forces, I flew a British Airways flight to John F. Kennedy Airport in New York. I checked two suitcases and a small carry-on. That was the extent of my belongings in terms of material wealth. So much has changed in my life since then, including the acquisition of material wealth in many different forms. Danielle and I are richly blessed, and we attribute all of it to God's goodness and grace, first and foremost. Wisdom, Knowledge, and Counsel have had a very big part in this process as well. I continually engage with them. If I liken the Holy Spirit and the seven spirits of God to "underwriters" in all the deals that have bought us material wealth, Honor has been the broker.

Most of what adorns our home, builds our accounts, and meets our family's needs as well as our desires has come through Honor. We own many things that have been given to us, not because we project need or demand that people pay their way into relationship with us. Things are given to us out of honor. I opt not to give examples here to maintain the confidentiality of precious moments when things of value were traded into our family.

By the same token, Danielle and I—and increasingly our children as well—pursue a lifestyle of honor. We are constantly looking for opportunities and developing systems by which we can give honor. At our church, we have four parking spaces designated for pastoral staff. Between 2010 and 2013, when we renovated our facility and set up the parking spots, I parked my car in the slot farthest to the right. In my opinion, it is the best place to park, because it is closest to the door and affords much space for opening my car doors without the chance of bumping into neighboring cars. When our family moved to Cyprus for the years 2013-2015, the parking space went to the man God raised up to serve as our church pastor, Tim d'Albenas. When we returned from Cyprus in the summer of 2015, I did not reclaim my parking space. I never park there, even if I know Tim will be out of town for an extended time.

During a large conference we hosted in 2016, Tim and his wife Robin were flying out for business on the last day of the event. Parking spaces were in high demand. I remember pulling up that morning and seeing Tim's space open, while all other pastoral spots were occupied. I continued to the back of the property and parked on the gravel. While I walked towards the building, one of the men attending the conference asked, "There was a spot right there, and you are a pastor. Why not park there?" Without thinking about it, I responded, "That's not a spot for parking. That's a spot for honor." I proceeded to explain what I meant. "That spot is Tim's regardless of whether he is here or not. It is a small way by which I honor him in my heart." The man's countenance changed. He was moved. He got it. The empty space conveyed Kingdom love and brotherhood. It was filled with God's glory—because it has been designated, by one son to another, for honor. Things like this are not done with much pre-calculation and planning. They are commonplace among us, as we have been cultivating honor as a lifestyle in our fellowship.

It would take another whole book to express how many people and moments of bestowing honor on individuals I carry in my heart. I often lay awake imagining such scenarios. I have had dreams and visions in which I honor people. Such encounters often end with me weeping before my Father, expressing my strong desire to be a vessel for honor. These are precious times with YHVH when I lay all plans and aspirations at His feet. I share this very intimate part of my walk with Him to indicate that the rewards of Honor come from a lifestyle of honor, and that lifestyle must be maintained. To whom much is given, much will be required. We have been given so much, because we have found favor with God and man as sons. I have dedicated my life to express honor in every way possible, especially through giving. I even asked the Lord to hire me as a full-time giver in His Kingdom. He knows I mean it. I hope you do, too.

I want to know as much as I can about honor—to walk in it and to be clothed with it. I desire to grow in my ability to leverage honor for the advancement of God's Kingdom. And that means learning not only how to give honor, but also how to receive it. Honor must flow unhindered by pride, inhibitions, or insecurities. Those who can only give honor, but cannot receive it, block it just as much as not being able to give it but only receive it. I think of myself as an overseer, whose job is to ensure the river's proper flow. Water comes from the high places, such as the mountains, and it runs by means of the river to the crops in the valley. I make sure it keeps flowing. It is that way with honor. We must keep honor flowing so it can flood the world that so desperately needs it.

Epilogue

I am often asked to give practical applications for the various concepts I put forth in my teachings and books. Perhaps I do not include such applications because I am failing somewhere in my ability to fully communicate the principles. I am willing to work on getting better in that regard.

I offer the following not as an excuse, but simply for your consideration. I struggle with including practical applications because so much of what I speak and write about comes out my personal relationship with God. I seek Him because I want just Him. Out of that pursuit comes the knowledge and revelation that often ends up in my books. It is hard to quantify or formularize my encounters. The dynamics of my upbringing, education, pursuit of Jesus, study of the Word, and the myriads of experiences that have taught me about honor are impossible to package in a few simple words.

With much respect and love for you, and with immense gratitude for your purchase and reading of this book, here is the best practical application I can come up with at this point in my development: To walk with Honor and reap from Honor, walk with YHVH. Passionately, diligently, and consistently seek Him. God will guide you and pave the way for you, teaching you everything you need to maximize your potential in Him. And let the few things that may have inspired or challenged you from this book be the diving board into a pool of prayer and pursuit.

We are victorious in Christ. Always! Glory to Glory!

Author's Bio

Marios Ellinas is an international speaker, author and consultant.

He has authored numerous inspirational books and two spy thrillers.

Marios lives in Connecticut, USA, with his wife and three children.